(BOOK ONE)

BONNY CAPPS

SNUFF (Book 1)

SNL[illegible] (Boo[illegible] 1)

WARNING

This book is not just dark—it's horrific, depraved and disturbing. If you do not enjoy books containing blood, guts, taboo and more, this book is not for you.

Acknowledgements

First, I want to thank my amazing husband and children for being so patient with me while I write my stories.

To the wonderful members of Gabe's Girls, you guys have so much more faith in me than I have in myself. Thank you for keeping my head above water and my vision clear.

I couldn't do anything without my incredible PA, Ebony Simone McMillan. I love you, sister. <3

Tara Dawn, my literary twin—you've become such an incredible friend, and you deal with my random midnight ramblings. Thank you for everything that you do for me—and thank you for editing this bad boy! Also, a big thank you for your parody making skills! I can't wait to write Twins this year. Stay in my head, and I'll stay in yours. I love your face! <3

To the lovely ladies that beta read this book: Sharon Sheeley, Wendy Wuttke, Agnese Maria Kohn, Amy Davis, Jamie Buchanan, Catherine Gray, Linda Marie Barrett, Sanne Heremans, Sara Gagnon, Melissa Mendoza, Angie Vogelzang, Diane Norwood, Phyl Drollett, Kylie Hillman, Kimberly Ervin-Echols and Nerdy Nadine—this book wouldn't be possible without your feedback. Thank you so much.

To my wonderful parents who have supported my dreams, your faith in me keeps me going. I love you guys.

My sister and biggest fan, Heather—I love you to the moon and back.

To everyone that's taken the time to read this story, thank you.

“Man is the cruelest animal.”

-FRIEDRICH NIETZSCHE

Chapter 1

Blood, Sweat and Sequins

SOFIA

"Alright Sofia, let's start with some spinning," Mirna, my coach says as she watches me with eagle eyes.

I nod as I allow my feet to glide to the center of the rink. The jarring sound of my skates grinding into the ice are audible over the upbeat music that streams from the speakers of the empty stadium.

"Left hip up!" Mirna demands softly. "Keep your thighs and feet tight!"

I lift my left leg and spread my arms as I welcome the spin.

"That's right, drive your heel down. Very good. Very, very good. Now finish," she says as I allow my body to gracefully come out of the spin.

She nods pointedly to the center of the ice. "Classic, side, and hair cutter."

I nod as I gracefully stride across the ice. I gain momentum as I enter into the spin before bending my left leg at the knee. Leaning back, I fall into classic position before leaning my head to the side. Then, I pull my foot up behind my head to perform the hair cutter.

Mirna claps her hands. “Yes! Your grace has improved immensely since your injury. How are you feeling?”

I smile as I approach her. “Much better now that the cast is off.”

“Well,” she says, placing her hands on her hips. “You keep this up, we may be able to make it to Nationals, yeah?”

I smile as I nod. “That would be amazing. I want to compete more than anything in the world.”

She places a hand on each of my arms before gently squeezing. “You’ve come a long way. The fact that you got up after that fall several months ago shows me everything. This is in your blood, Sofia. Not that I’ve ever doubted it.”

Looking down at my skates, I blush.

“Are you up for any jumps? Maybe a half turn or a single?”

I flash her a toothy grin. "How about a double?"

Her eyebrows sit high on her forehead. "A double? Do you think you're up to it?"

"I think so. I've got to prepare. Nationals are six months away. I can't miss it."

She smiles, releasing me. "Alright, then. Show me what you've got."

Months ago, I was at competition performing to a shortened version of Smetana's *Die Moldau*. When I didn't land the triple jump, I rolled onto my ankle. I still swear to this day that I heard the bone snap over the powerful melody. I knew that I had hurt myself badly—especially when your feet are your life.

The only thing that made me get back up was the music streaming through the speakers as the audience silently looked on. I got up because of Smetana and his drive to never stop creating masterpieces regardless of not being able to hear them. He was deaf, but he never gave up on his music. Music was his art … skating is mine.

I attempted to stand, and when the pain shot up my leg, I fell to my side. Finally, I stood on one shaking leg and managed to push off with my wounded one. I finished the song, and I smiled when red roses rained down around my feet. I didn't win that competition, but I finished it. That's what matters.

My mother and I are both equally passionate about my sport. I was tiny the first time that she laced up my first pair of skates. I clumsily tried to straighten my stubby, toddler legs when I first felt the slick ice beneath me.

The rink became my entirety. Soon, I came to glide effortlessly. Then came the spins and the jumps.

I train over twenty hours a week. When I'm not practicing at the stadium with Mirna, I'm at the ballet studio or the gym.

When you're a figure skater, you must have the agility of a speed skater, the strength of a hockey player, and the grace of a ballerina. The sport is a mystery to most who watch. What the audience sees is a beautiful girl effortlessly gliding and leaping. They don't see the blood and sweat. That's how it's meant to be. If it looks strenuous, the art is ruined. There is only room for perfection. The best feeling in the world is an effortless program; all of your choreographed steps neatly executed as an audience looks on with starry eyes.

I'm sixteen years old, and I've been skating for twelve years. My one wish in life is to compete nationally for the US. Though I'm of Russian descent, I was born in the states. My mother and I have moved seven times since I can remember. It was odd for me to remain at the same school for an extended period of time. So, every year, I had to combat the stares that I got when I was introduced at a new school. My fellow classmates thought it odd when a foreign looking Sofia Dmitriev was introduced, then when they didn't hear a trace of an accent, the questions would pour from their mouths like water from a vase.

"What's up with your name?"

"Are you from here?"

"You sound American ... are you American?"

I've never really fit in because of that reason. When I'm not on the ice, I prefer to stay to myself.

My mother is a doctor—a successful one, regardless of our countless moves across the country. Finally, we settled down in St. Louis. I have to say, it's my favorite to date with its old antique buildings; some with statues that sit atop them. I guess my mother likes it, too, because we've lived here for over three years, which is a record.

I make it to our townhouse, which is a short walk from the Stadium where I practice.

"Mom?" I holler from the entryway as I throw my saddle bag beside the shoe rack.

"In here!" she yells from the kitchen. I'm relieved that she actually isn't working tonight. It's a rarity to have her home since she's always on call.

I smell something burning as I approach the kitchen and smile when I see her waving an oven mitten around. Smoke billows from the open oven as she pulls out a pan with something burnt to a crisp. I can't make-out what it is.

I laugh. "What are you making … or, what *were* you trying to make?"

She shakes her head slowly before taking a sip of her wine. "I wish that I would have paid more attention when mama tried to teach me her recipes."

Sliding onto the barstool, I rest my chin on my hands. "I could have cooked."

My mother rolls her eyes as she places her hands on her hips. "For once, I wanted to make you dinner. It's okay. Chinese it is."

She places her elbows on the wooden island before propping her chin on her hands. “Mirna said you did phenomenal today, my love. You’ve been working so hard.”

She pauses as she reaches down behind the counter and retrieves a package.

She slides the silver and black wrapped gift toward me before tapping it with her index finger.

“What is this?” I whisper as I run my finger along the black, silk bow.

She grabs my hand and presses it to her lips. I try not to become emotional as I watch her proud eyes fill with tears.

“I am so proud of you, Sofia. You couldn’t be any more perfect. You’re a dream come true. Your papa … he would have been very proud.”

I blink to clear the tears that have collected in my eyes.

“Go on,” she pressures. “Open it.”

Sliding the present across the table, I gently unfold the wrapping paper to expose a brown box. When I lift the lid, my eyes grow wide.

"Mama, these are four hundred dollar skates!"

My eyes snap to her cognac colored gaze. "Only the best for my princess, yeah? The blades are also top of the market."

Her slight Russian accent is airy and light. Her words always warm my soul.

"Thank you, Mama. So much."

She sniffles as she runs her hands over her teary eyes. "Enough of that. Let's go get some food."

Chapter 2

Hungry Dreams

6 Months Later

When you want something badly enough, your soul craves it. You could starve for days to achieve it. The climb is just the beginning. Finishing … that's where you feel success, and I'm not planning on taking a fall again. Not anytime soon.

I only feel comfortable on the ice. When the music possesses me and my body seemingly becomes a note in a song.

The stadium is dark as *Big Eyes* by Lana Del Rey streams through the speakers above. The surrounding space is black, and the spotlight is on me as I pretend an audience is watching. My mother doesn't know—and Mirna doesn't either—that I've been practicing my triple jump. My ankle is still weak, but I can do this. At sixteen years old, the perfect triple is almost unheard of.

Today, I've fallen twice, but I almost landed after the third try. What I wouldn't give to land that triple jump and find my mother amongst the others in the audience smiling proudly. It would be perfection … it would be *priceless*.

Lana's melodic voice blankets me as the blades of my skates slice into the ice. My body feels weightless as I circle the rink with my arms out. My eyes are closed as I feel the music in my very *soul*.

Work. Never-ending work. I know the end game, so giving up isn't a choice. My legs are on fire from the relentless squats, jogging, and other horrible exercises that I inflict on them.

I stumble when I reach the last step of the bleachers and place my hands on my knees as I catch my breath.

I see a pair of cleats appear in my line of sight and my eyes work their way up the legs, to an abdomen, and … to a handsome, familiar face.

Standing straight, I place my hands on my hips as my breaths furiously work their way in and out of my lungs.

"You're that Russian girl," Brent Masterson says as a broad smile covers his face, showcasing a deep dimple in his cheek.

I roll my eyes as I begin to jog around the soccer field. It doesn't take long for him to catch up.

"You are Russian, right? I'm just saying that because it's what I've heard."

I smirk. "I'm American. I was born here."

He keeps with my pace as I round the soccer field.

"That's cool."

I stop suddenly and turn to face him. "What do you want?"

Looking over his shoulder, I see his fellow teammates have paused their training as they stare at us. My eyes snap back to his. "I need to finish up my workout."

He smiles sheepishly. "I thought maybe you and I … I don't know, we could catch a movie or something."

I smile as I turn on my heel and continue on my way.

"Not a chance!" I holler.

"You have to go out with him!" Mirna exclaims as the hairstylist finishes up my hair.

I laugh. "Absolutely not!"

"Why?" she implores.

"Because, he's not my type," I respond as the hairstylist pats my shoulder, letting me know that she's finished with me.

"And, what is your type?"

I scoff as I turn to face her. "Not him. He's popular … and wealthy. He doesn't know anything about anything."

"Dumb jock," she remarks and I nod emphatically.

"Well," she continues, "I think you should try and date. You're sixteen going on seventeen. I know skating is important, but I don't think it should impede on your teenage years as much as you've allowed it to."

"Says my coach," I retort.

She smiles fondly. "And your friend. I've known you since you were tiny. Your mother is a dear friend of mine, so naturally I feel a little more for you than your average coach."

"Speaking of," I say, slipping my phone out of my bag. "I haven't heard from mom. Has she texted you or called?"

Mirna smiles as she shakes her head. "Not yet, but you know your mom. She probably is making it here by the skin of her teeth. I bet she's just getting off the plane."

I nod as a fond smile spreads over my face. She's right. Mom is always fashionably late, but I know she wouldn't miss this. I've been waiting for my chance to compete at Nationals. I know she'll be here right in time to see my performance.

My heart pounds against my chest as I watch another skater perform. I'm next.

I shake my hands in front of me before hopping from one foot to the other to keep myself warm for my program. I look around and see others practicing their steps. Some are singles, like me, and others are couples.

I spot Mirna before approaching her.

"I'm freaking out," I breathe out.

Smiling, she grasps my shoulders before giving them a squeeze. "You'll be incredible. Don't psyche yourself out."

"Can I see your phone?" I ask, and she nods before placing it in my hand.

"Make it quick. You go up in five."

I nod as I step away from her and dial my mother's number.

"You've reached Dr. Lidiya Dmitriev. I'm busy, but leave me a message and I'll call you back."

Squeezing my eyes shut, I try and speak past the lump in my throat.

"Mommy, it's me," I whisper as my eyes spring open and dart around frantically. "I'm going up soon. I hope you're here when I do. I love you."

Handing the phone back to Mirna, she squeezes my cheek lovingly before slapping my butt.

It's time.

I close my eyes as I drift across the ice to the center and pose, awaiting the song that will accompany my program.

Once Blackmill's *Evil Beauty* begins to play, I become something different; a duckling that transforms into a graceful swan, full of beauty and confidence. The sheer white skirt whispers against my thighs as I prepare for an axle jump. When I drift half circle, I kick off and spin effortlessly before landing.

The set is going exactly as planned until it comes time to execute the triple that I've been practicing for months. This was meant for my mom and Mirna, but I can't look toward the audience, because I know either way, whether or not she's there watching me or if she didn't make it … it would only serve as a distraction. I've been training non-stop for my moment—*for this moment.*

I glide across the ice, spinning several times to build up the momentum that I need to execute this jump. When I'm airborne, I spin three times before landing perfectly. My heart soars, and I'm sure my pride is evident on my face. I imagine Mirna and mom smiling from ear to ear as I conclude my flawless set.

Crossing my legs and lifting my arms, I welcome the cheering audience.

I did it.

I look into Mirna's eyes, and my smile immediately falls when I see her distraught appearance.

A police officer stands beside her as she clutches a large teddy bear and sobs into its faux fur. My mother is nowhere to be seen, and the world closes in on me as I fall to my knees onto the sea of roses that had been thrown at my feet.

Chapter 3

The Worst Goodbye

Mirna clutches my hand as my mother's attorney reads off her will.

Her funeral was two days ago as rain poured from the heavens. She always called rain angel tears, and I guess that hit home more than anything. So many attended, and they all looked toward me solemnly. There I was ... an orphan … parentless in an ongoing world. It never slowed down, not even when the most amazing person I've ever known had been stolen too soon.

Everyone went home afterward and lived their lives while my tears never let up. There I was in our empty home, walking the halls aimlessly and smelling her clothing.

She was struck by a car as she frantically tried to make it across the street to the stadium where I performed. While I was in my happy place, she was taken from me.

The attorney's words mean nothing. Yes, she left me everything, but I'd gladly live on the street if it only meant that I could see her one last time.

"Sofia," the attorney says as his eyes flit from the will and then to me. "Do you know of your uncle? He lives in Russia. His name is Artur Ivanov. He is your mother's brother."

I shake my head slowly as I stare blankly at his intricately carved mahogany desk.

"I'm sorry," I whisper. "I've never heard of him."

He clears his throat as he sits back in his chair. "It was your mother's wish that you go and stay with him."

"What?" Mirna breathes out. "Absolutely not. She can stay with me."

I hold a hand up as my gaze slowly meets his. "It was her wish?"

He nods slowly. "It was."

"Do I have to go?"

He shakes his head. "We can work something out. If you wish to stay here—"

"No," I interrupt. "If it was her wish, then I will go."

"Sofia! It's Russia!" Mirna exclaims, tightening her grip on my hand.

I yank my hand from hers and ball my fists in my lap. "She wanted me to go. I appreciate your offer, but I have to do what she wanted."

"It's Russia. You've never been there. It could be dangerous. Here, you'll be with me. You can continue to skate and go to school where you're familiar."

I shake my head as my eyes find hers. I frown when I look into her pleading eyes before my gaze drifts back to my lap.

"Where? Where in Russia does he live?" I ask.

"Mezmay … it's a small village, some twenty-three hours plus from Moscow." He pauses as he opens the desk drawer and retrieves an envelope.

"This was included in her will. It's a letter. For you."

Chapter 4

A Letter and Change

My father died when I was very young. The only memories that I have is of him handing me sweets as I sat on the floor beside his armchair while he watched the daily news and I played with dolls.

He died from a sudden brain aneurysm. Just like my mother, his death was quick and unexpected, leaving more questions than answers to those left behind.

The letter that my mother had written almost seemed as though she had already planned her untimely death. She knew that I'd become an orphan, or perhaps she thought it was better safe than sorry. Knowing her, she'd probably written the same letter over and over at the dawn of each New Year. She didn't want me to be alone. Maybe this letter is her way of staying … speaking to me from beyond the grave.

I read my dead mother's words each time I boarded a new flight to get to where I am now. I wouldn't wish the ten plus hour journey on my worst enemy.

As I sit in the train, I stare out into the vast beauty that is Russia. From the rolling hills to the snowcapped mountains that stand tall in the distance, I know she wanted me to experience my roots.

I'm in for another twenty-four hours of travel to get from Moscow to Sochi, where my uncle awaits. Then, we have an hour and a half to drive to get to Mezmay. I'd take this train ride over flying anytime. It's much more comfortable and roomy. Not to mention, I prefer the breathtaking scenery compared to the tiny patches of land below as the plane soared through the clouds.

I hold my mother's folded letter in my lap. I've read it a thousand times and I'll probably read it a thousand more. I'll try to find something hidden in between the lines like I already have numerous times. I'll cry, allowing more tears to smudge the ink that swirls into her beautiful handwriting.

It's summer, which I'm thankful for. Russia is infamous for its brutally cold winters. Mirna moved into our townhouse until school was out, then I boarded a plane and left.

Since landing in Moscow, I've learned that younger Russians speak English, while the middle aged to elderly either don't, or they just don't want to speak to me. I don't know a lick of Russian, so the fact that my mother was so set on me coming here is interesting to say the least. She never taught me about the culture or the language.

Smiling, waving, and small talk aren't a thing here. I've tried and have been ignored several times, unless it's a boy my age. They tend to smile and talk excessively. I've gotten some raised eyebrows from girls and women, and I believe it's because of my lazy attire involving yoga pants and my blonde hair in a bun. High fashion *is* definitely a thing here.

I turned seventeen several months ago. It was the loneliest and most heartbroken that I've felt since mom passed away. Our annual tradition of Indian food and ice-cream died when she did.

I'm happy to be alone in this cab. It's just me, the choppy sound the train makes as it thunders down the tracks, and my dead mother's words.

Placing the letter beside me, I open the window of the cab and lean out.

My hair tickles my face as I inhale the fresh air, allowing myself to feel something. Because I've been so numb. I've allowed myself to curl up into my shell. Maybe mom was right.

Maybe I needed this shock after she was taken away.

Once I retrieve my luggage, I look up and down the eerily vacant platform of the train station as the train begins tugging along once more. Nobody else got off. It seems that I'm all alone here, and for a moment my heart skips a beat. Then, I see a man approaching me. He's holding up a sign as he points excitedly to the words that I cannot understand. He's smiling, and his face is familiar … his brown eyes and crooked smile resemble my mother's.

This is my uncle.

I place my luggage on each side of me before stepping forward. I lift my hand and wave shyly. This entire encounter is so awkward.

Holding his hands out to his sides, a wide grin spreads across his face. "Sofia?"

It makes me smile; his heavy Russian accent and how he emphasized the "a" at the end.

I nod. "Uncle Artur?"

He rushes over to me, and for a moment I think he will hug me, but then he grabs my luggage and turns hastily.

I'm left standing before I hurry after him, my legs moving quickly to keep up with his pace.

He approaches a very small car and opens the hatchback before hurling my suitcases in the back. I bite the inside of my cheek and cringe when I think about my breakables. Then, he gets into the driver's side. I stand awkwardly—stunned by this strange reunion. I snap out of it when he begins honking his horn repeatedly.

I hurriedly slide into the passenger seat and I'm barely able to close the door when the engine sputters to life and we're on our way.

I don't say a word when we turn onto a winding, dirt road. This village is tiny. Something that you would only see on the Travel Channel on a boring weekday night.

Goats with curled horns stand on their hind legs to reach the bushes on the other side of the fence. Chickens scurry across the road before we pass and cows graze freely with bells hung from their necks.

The foliage is lush and the trees stand tall around the village. The fences are painted bright blue and the windows are open to display the simple, yet cluttered interiors of the tiny homes.

Uncle Artur has his arm rested on the open window and lazily lifts his hand occasionally to acknowledge the other villagers.

"Ah! Here we are," he says as he pulls up to a tiny home.

I look up through the windshield and see the yellow painted wooden structure. It looks cozy. A mare and her foal look at us over the fence as if to greet us.

I reach for the handle and the door creaks open before I step out and inhale the fresh air. I feel like my lungs are being cleansed with each inhale of crisp, pure air.

I step toward the house as he grabs my luggage from the back. He steps beside me and sighs.

"Your mama grew up here," he mumbles before he begins walking to the front door. That alone sparks my curiosity, and I hurry after him.

"This was your childhood home?" I ask as the front door swings open.

He nods. "Ya. This was Mama and Papa's home."

I tilt my head, suddenly realizing that he speaks fairly good English. He didn't utter a word the entire drive.

"This is your room," he says as he stomps down the hall and disappears through a door.

I walk behind him and watch as he places my bags on the rickety, metal bed.

He exits and disappears down the hall into the kitchen area.

"Thank you!" I holler as I make my way further into the room.

My eyes travel from the bed which has a colorful quilt to the antique clock that hangs from the wall then to the desk. The old, wooden floors creak with each step that I take.

"I'll have dinner ready in a little while, okay?"

I startle before turning to face him. "Thanks."

"It okay?" he asks, and I look around the room before my eyes travel back to him.

"It's perfect. Thank you."

He nods before tucking his hands in his pockets. I can tell by the deep wrinkles in his face and his calloused hands that he's a hard worker. I don't think there's much of a choice when you live in a place like this.

"I go tend to the animals. You settle in," he says as he turns and leaves me alone.

He's certainly flighty and enigmatic. His hurried movements make me nervous.

Plopping down on the bed, I watch out the window as he shoos the horses away once he enters the pasture. Wrapping my arms around my shoulders, I shiver. It must be about fifty degrees out there—in the middle of summer, might I add.

I turn to my luggage and slowly unzip the smaller suitcase. I carefully pick up the picture of my mother and me, thankful that the glass frame wasn't broken when he hurled my luggage into the trunk earlier.

Smiling, I trace my fingers over my mother's smiling face. We're both smiling from ear to ear. My skates hang over my shoulder and the vacant ice rink is in the background. I sigh as a solitary tear creeps down my cheek before I quickly wipe it away.

Placing the picture on the nightstand, I press my fingers to my lips before placing them over my mother's picture.

"I love you, Mom."

Two Weeks Later

There's a boy. I don't know his name, but I first saw him when I was lying in the purple wildflowers that grow on the outskirts of the village.

I was staring up at the scattered clouds when I heard something rustling beside me. I sat up quickly and peered over the tall flowers to see brown eyes staring back at me. He leapt up and ran. I followed hastily, eager to befriend someone my age. Most of the villagers are my uncle's age, and *none* of them speak English.

I was on the boy's heels, but he disappeared into the lush wilderness, leaving me alone at a breathtaking waterfall. I clumsily sat down on a rock and watched in awe as the water tumbled down to the river below. I closed my eyes and listened intently to the majestic sounds that nature offered. I allowed myself peace. I allowed myself to breathe.

The second time that I saw the boy was when he was pushing a wheelbarrow several houses down from my uncle's. He caught me and I leapt behind a tree. Peeking around, I saw a smile spread across his face.

I smiled, too, when I leaned against the tree and looked up toward the heavens.

Chapter 5

The Coldest Winter

Five Months Later

The horses watch me as I glide across the frozen pond. Snow falls gracefully from the sky as I lift my leg and spin effortlessly. My white jacket and gloves keep me warm as my hair whispers across my face. It's the most freeing feeling in the world.

The music streams through my headphones that are kept in place by my furry earmuffs. My face is freezing, and I'm sure that the tip of my nose is bright red, but I don't care. I needed this abandon. I haven't skated since mom died, but the sudden urge that I felt an hour ago told me everything that I needed to know.

She said it in the letter, and I swear that it was her whispering in my ear when I looked at the skates that she bought me as they hung from the wall.

Never give up, my love ….

I've been eyeing this pond for some time, and I was thankful when it finally froze over. It's behind the boy's house.

Closing my eyes, I open my arms and welcome the melody. The ice is my destiny, and the moon is my friend. The music though … the music is my inspiration.

When the song comes to an end, I gracefully lift my arms above me and smile.

However, the rendezvous between me and the ice soon comes to an end when I hear clapping in the distance.

My eyes dart open and I see the boy.

"You," I murmur as I glide toward him. He doesn't run away this time.

Running a hand over his head, he smiles.

"I didn't know you were an ice princess," he says playfully.

I laugh. "An ice princess?"

He nods. "My name is Boris."

"I'm Sofia," I say, reaching out to shake his hand.

He gives me a crooked smile before he removes his glove with his left hand. Then, he nods to mine.

I look down at my gloved hand before my eyes travel back to his.

"What?"

He laughs. "Nothing says foreigner like wearing a glove when shaking hands in Russia."

I cock my head. "I'm not following."

Rolling his eyes, he grabs my hand and shakes it. "You're American?"

I yank my hand from his, allowing it to fall to my side. "My parents were Russian."

He nods. "Were?"

Looking down at the ice, I sigh. "Yeah. *Were*."

"Boris!" A voice hollers from the back door of his home.

I look over his shoulder and frown at the intimidating man that approaches us. He doesn't look like the others in the village. He looks scary. He looks *dangerous*.

“I’ve got to go,” Boris says, quickly turning. But the man grabs his shoulder and turns him back around.

“Where are you going little brother? You can’t introduce your brother to this beautiful girl? I’m only here for a couple of days. What gives?”

I blush as I nervously look toward my uncle’s house. I see Uncle Artur standing in the doorway with both hands on the doorframe.

“This is Sofia. Sofia, this is my brother Vadim.”

My eyes snap to the man and I take a moment to examine him before removing my glove to shake his hand. He has a shaved head and there is a deep scar running through his eyebrow. His hooded eyes are so dark that they almost look black.

I swallow the lump in my throat as I reach out and place my hand in his. “Nice to meet you.”

The warmth of his hand engulfs mine and he squeezes tightly … showing me his power … showing me that he is a man that is not to be crossed. When I try and take my hand from his, he doesn’t allow it. Instead, he runs a thumb over the top of my hand, causing my heart to beat erratically beneath my ribs.

“Sofia!” My uncle bellows from the doorway, and that makes Vadim release me. I quickly back away, almost losing my footing on the ice. Vadim laughs darkly as he places a hand on Boris' shoulder, and I take note of the tattoos that spread across his knuckles. Boris flinches when Vadim noticeably squeezes his shoulder.

"I hope that I see you soon, *krasivaya,*" he says, before he turns and drags Boris behind him to their house.

I stand frozen in place before my uncle hollers my name once more.

Several days have passed since that awkward encounter between Boris, Vadim, and I. My uncle didn't seem happy about me speaking to them one bit. I don't know why.

I spend my days helping my uncle on the farm. I had no wish to go to school here, so I was sure to bring my senior curriculum with me to study. I never felt like I belonged in school anyway. I like my solitary existence. At least for now. It's just me, nature, and my odd uncle who I know nothing about. He isn't affectionate, nor is he very talkative.

He goes about his days crafting and doing other random things around the farm.

At first, winter here was beautiful. But now, it only reminds me how alone I am.

Boris won't even look at me anymore, but Vadim … I see his black eyes constantly watching me. He frightens me. I don't think he's a nice person, and I've never been the judgmental type. I give everyone an equal opportunity, regardless of what they look like. My mother taught me that. She wouldn't hesitate to help anyone, regardless of where they came from.

She used to say, "Looks don't matter, Sofia. It's what's in the heart and the mind. Looks, they just tell a fraction of the story. A man who fought a war may wear rags, and a businessman with a suit and tie may have stolen to get where he is now."

Vadim, he looks at me like I'm a steak on a platter. Looks alone, I'd say he is dangerous. But it's his demeanor that frightens me the most.

Rolling up the rug in my room, I put it up to the wall before I plug my head phones in and turn my MP3 player onto mellow music.

I practice my steps as I sway from side to side, following the same steps of the set that I performed at Nationals. My *winning* set. Though, I didn't win anything that fateful night. Instead, I lost everything.

I'm mid spin when I hear a loud bang. I rip my earbuds from my ears and stand still.

I stay like that, listening to the silence.

Walking to the door, I open it slowly and peek down the hallway. Everything seems in its place as I tiptoe down the hallway.

"Uncle Artur?" I whisper.

My eyes grow wide when I see a crimson puddle growing wider the further I get down the hall.

I gasp when I see his face. His eyes are wide and lifeless as the blood trickles from what looks to be a bullet wound between his eyes.

"Oh my God!" I scream.

I attempt to turn and run, but an arm wraps around my shoulders before I feel a painful prick in my neck.

My eyelids become heavy and my lips move slowly, but I'm not sure if I'm making a sound. My uncle's lifeless body becomes blurry as my body goes slack in the unknown arms.

I struggle, but it seems useless. The only thing that I can feel are the warm tears as they slither down my cheeks, and the only thing that I can hear is the slow rhythm of my heart as my world goes black.

Chapter 6

The Place we go to Die

I feel like I'm floating in a sea of nothingness. My eyes open occasionally, and all that I can see are blurs and colors, nothing more. I can hear voices, but they're lost in the confusion.

I'm not sure how much time passes while I'm in this state. It feels like a dream. I could be swimming in lucid unconsciousness for all I know.

Yes. This is a dream. It must be. I'll wake up soon.

The thought makes me smile. I think I'm smiling, at least. You can never tell in dreams.

My body is abruptly lifted and it makes my head spin. I feel something cold against my feet before being yanked forward. I believe that I'm putting one foot after the other, but I'm not sure.

I look up and see the stars before my eyes and clumsily look toward what seems to be a mansion. From there, my gaze drops further to a man's back. He's pulling a rope, and when my eyes follow it, I realize that it's tied around my wrists.

He's pulling me, yet for some reason, I can't struggle against him.

I close my eyes for a moment, but when I open them, I'm no longer outside.

I'm walking through a long hallway. As my eyes travel to my surroundings, I see rooms on each side. Some have curtains pulled to the side, and others are closed. The rooms that are opened have people inside of them. I can't make it out. I do hear screams, though, and I'm sure that there is blood on the floor. Again, I try to struggle and run, but I can't.

Yes, because you are dreaming, Sofia.

Cold. Something cold beneath me. I hear my heartbeat in my ears and my body is sorer than it's ever been. The ache in my muscles and bones is excruciating. I haven't felt this sore even after rigorously working out to prepare for Nationals.

My mind is fuzzy, and each time I try and will my eyelids to open, I'm unsuccessful. My body feels heavy, unlike the dream that I had where I was seemingly floating.

I'm afraid that I'm still dreaming. I must be. But in dreams, can you smell your surroundings? I don't think you can. I smell what can only be described as filth. Damp, dirty, filth.

I hear voices too. They are low, and the tongue is foreign. They are speaking Russian. I know that much because I've been studying the language since I've been here.

I can only make out certain words, *"the girl"* and *"fresh meat."* Those are not the words that I wish to hear. I can only hope that the dream has turned to a nightmare and that I'm soon to wake-up and escape from the dark recesses of my mind.

I lay like this for some time as my body slowly comes back to life. My head is no longer spinning and the numbness that was once so inviting leaves me to the dreaded realization that this isn't a dream.

I recall the events that led me here, and I allow the tears to seep out from below my closed eyelids. Blood … Uncle Artur lifeless on the floor … the sudden prick in my neck before my world turned into one big blur.

I don't know where I am. I don't know who took me. All I know is that I'm hundreds and hundreds of miles from home.

Alone.

I hear footsteps approaching, but I'm afraid to move or open my eyes for fear of what I might find. I know deep in my heart that my life has changed for the worst, and I'm afraid that it may be for good.

The footsteps stop and my breathing slows. I'm sure that I'm noticeably trembling, but I can only hope that this person doesn't notice. If they do, I'm afraid that they will hurt me.

The footsteps begin again, but this time they get farther away before I hear a door open and close. Then, I'm left in the silence once more.

My eyes crack open, just enough to allow me to make out my surroundings. Panic courses throughout my body when I realize that I am in a cage fit for a large parrot. There are other cages, but only one other is occupied. It's a boy. A skinny boy who looks no older than twelve or thirteen.

He lies on his side in a deep sleep. His bones protrude through his clothing, and I swear that I can count every single rib on his tiny body.

A dripping sound echoes throughout the concrete room and my eyes travel to a hose. My eyes follow it and I find the faucet where the water drips steadily to the cold floor below.

My breaths become hurried as I frantically sit up on my hands and knees. I can barely lift my head in this cage as my hands search erratically for an escape.

"You're awake."

I freeze when I hear the tiny voice, and my eyes travel to the boy as he rubs his sleepy eyes.

I crawl to him hastily and grasp the metal bars tightly as my eyes frantically search his face. "Where am I? What is this place?"

He looks toward me solemnly before his gaze drops to his lap. "They tell me nothing good about this place. They say this is the place we go to die," he murmurs in broken English.

I don't recognize his accent, and I find myself searching his face to determine where he's from, but I can't. I don't have enough time, because once again, the door flings open.

I scramble to the back of the cage, trying to get as far away as possible, but that's impossible with the metal bars digging into my back.

My heart threatens to beat from my chest as I watch the man bend down and retrieve the hose from the ground. He pinches it as he turns on the faucet, then he approaches me.

He kneels down, and I immediately recognize his face.

"V—Vadim?" I squeak out as I look up at him through bleary eyes.

A dark grin spreads across his face as he narrows his black eyes at me. I can see my terrified reflection in his gaze when he says, "Welcome home, *krasivaya.*"

Then, all I feel is the ice cold water as he sprays me down.

I scream as loud as I can, and each time I do, he aims the hose at my mouth, causing me to cough relentlessly.

Eventually, I stop screaming as I curl into myself.

I'm so cold. Not only on the outside, but the inside as well. The skinny boy's words ring in my ears when Vadim finally stops hosing me down and leaves us alone once more in our cages.

"They say this is the place we go to die."

Chapter 7

The Devil is Real

It's been almost a year since my mother died.

It's been months since I came to Russia.

It's been six days since my uncle was killed.

It's been six days since I've been imprisoned.

It is the same routine every day. The boy is silent. He won't say his name or where he's from. The only thing he's ever said to me is that this is the place we go to die. I didn't believe him at first. I didn't want to, but now I'm afraid that he's right.

Every day, Vadim comes in and sprays us each down with the cold water before offering a bite of bread. He has a full loaf, but that's all he ever offers. One solitary bite. It isn't enough to calm our hungry stomachs. It is only enough to tease us. I've wanted so badly to yank the loaf from him, but that's impossible to do through the narrow bars of this cage. He'll allow us to use the bathroom once a day. The embarrassment got the better of me the first time when I refused to use the toilet in the corner of the room. However, when I pissed myself, the embarrassment magnified. Needless to say, I didn't turn down another "piss break," as Vadim calls it.

He's cruel, and I wonder how many other cruel men there are outside of this prison. I know there are more, because I heard them that first night.

I wonder how long the skinny boy has been here. I occasionally begin to feel bad for myself, but then I stop myself when I look at his frail body. Water is the only thing that's keeping us both alive, and we only get that when Vadim sprays us down as he taunts, "Drink up!"

My head hurts from the lack of nourishment and my body is so incredibly weak. It's hard to struggle. It's hard to move. At this point, it's becoming hard to *live*.

Today started off like the others. I feel as though I'm losing my grasp on reality. I find myself whispering *"Not today"* repeatedly, because I never know when my life will end. The idea is evident. No escape is in sight.

The door opens wide, but, this time, Vadim is not alone. He is followed by a lean, muscular man. This man's appearance is disheveled. His brown hair is messy, and his dark, cognac eyes immediately latch onto mine. The tight, white tank top that he wears is sprinkled with blood—and I can make out a nautical star tattoo on each of his shoulders. He is tall, standing several inches above Vadim, and his muscular body is intimidating.

He saunters over to me slowly before kneeling down on his haunches. He takes a drag of his cigarette before blowing it in my face.

I don't blink. I don't budge. I'm entranced by this dangerously handsome man as he kneels before me, drinking me in with his eyes alone.

"Him," he says to Vadim, his eyes never leaving mine.

My eyes snap to the skinny boy as Vadim approaches him. "No!" I exclaim as I watch him yank the boy from the cage.

The boy doesn't fight back, and I know it's because he's too weak.

My breaths become frantic as I rattle the bars of my cage. "Leave him alone! Please!"

Nobody bats an eye, not even the boy as his solemn eyes find mine one last time before he is dragged from the room.

I slump down as the sobs rack through my body. “Why?” I wail repeatedly.

The man still kneels before me as he smokes his cigarette. He watches me while I come undone, but he seems to care less.

When voice becomes raw, I can’t scream anymore. My chest shakes with each silent sob as I stare at the boy’s empty cage.

The man remains. He doesn’t say a word. He just watches and waits. I dare myself to look into his impassive gaze.

“Why am I here?” I rasp as I slowly sit up.

He runs a hand over his face, but doesn’t answer when Vadim comes into the room once more. Standing abruptly, he approaches Vadim and whispers something in his ear. Vadim doesn’t look enthused as he throws his hands up and says something in Russian. He’s talking so fast I can’t make out the words.

The man quickly grabs Vadim around the throat before slamming him against the wall. Again, I can’t make out what they are saying, their voices are so low.

The man leaves and Vadim narrows his eyes at me.

I cower in the cage as he stalks toward me. He yanks me from the cage and throws me down at his feet before tangling his fingers in my hair and yanking my head back.

"This is your lucky day, but believe me when I say—it is only a matter of time," he breathes into my ear before I'm jerked from the ground and dragged from the room.

My eyes travel around the white, tiled bathroom. It's clean, almost to the point of sterilization. The bleach burns my nose.

I wrap my arms around myself as I turn to face Vadim.

"What do you want me to do?"

He smiles wickedly as he nods to the shower. My gaze follows his as I nod my head slowly. "Okay, I'll shower. Alone."

He chuckles before lighting a cigarette. "I'm staying right here."

My eyes flit from the door and then back to him. I'm out of the cage. This has to be my only chance to escape. I don't know where to run, but it's worth a shot.

"You want to run? Go ahead? Just hope that I catch you before Andrei or Vlad. They would love to play with you, little American doll." He runs the hot end of the cigarette against the tile wall before successfully flicking it into the toilet. "Little American dolls are worth a lot of money. My cousin is an idiot for deciding to keep you. You were perfect for the next tape. Now I'll need to find another blonde American to take your place."

"T–tape?" I whisper as my eyes grow wide.

A depraved smile spreads across his face. "Yes," he whispers as he slowly approaches me. "The tape. You were meant to be the star. The best that I've ever captured."

I back into the cold wall as he gets closer and closer. His chest crushes mine and I feel his breath spread over my neck. "I wonder what your cold, lifeless body would look like. I wonder what words would be the last to whisper from your lips … I wonder …."

I shudder as a tear rolls down my cheek.

He steps back and looks down at me with those black eyes. "And I will continue to wonder, *krasivaya.* If you are a smart girl, you will not run. If you run, you will die."

"Why? Why are you doing this? I've never done anything to you," I rasp.

He smiles. "Why? Why what? Take you? That's simple."

I tilt my head as I watch his expression darken before he whispers, "Because I wanted to."

I'm sitting in a room. This room is dark, other than the fire that flickers across the way, but I'm still freezing as the remaining rivulets of water stream from my blonde locks before dripping onto the black silk robe that Vadim had me wear.

The room is decorated much like the rest of this place. I can barely remember what the exterior looked like when I was originally brought here, but the interior is classic. It's worlds away from the cage that I was imprisoned in below this home's mahogany floors.

Tall paintings line the halls of different men. They all look powerful and intimidating. Based on their clothing alone, I can tell they each come from different eras in time.

There are antique Soumak rugs strategically placed throughout this home and almost every room that I've seen has a fireplace with a blazing, roaring fire. The wooden floors are polished to perfection and numerous statues, vases, and other pieces of art are showcased throughout.

The room that I'm currently occupying is full of beautiful antiques. The bed alone is probably worth more money than I can even imagine. The four carved posts stand tall, almost touching the ceiling as a white, sheer fabric hangs down surrounding the bed.

I trace my fingers over one particular piece of furniture; a desk. I believe they call this style marquetry … beautifully crafted from various colored pieces of wood. The design is intricate. A skilled craftsman made this, and I notice many of the other pieces are of the same design. The desk is smooth to the touch, and shiny to the point that I can see the outline of my reflection.

My eyes travel to a large tapestry which hangs from the wall. It looks like a coat of arms; a two headed bird with a crest in the middle stitched with gold thread.

I walk to the window and peer out. This place is enormous. I think I'm several stories up, so jumping is definitely out of the question. The ground below is covered in snow and there is a metal privacy fence—too tall to climb—surrounding this place. Though, that's not what would render my escape. No. It's the armed men who are obviously patrolling the place.

"Where am I?" I whisper to myself.

So many questions circulate in my head as I watch the snow fall beyond the glass of my prison. Why did they kill my uncle and take me? What happened to the skinny boy? What tape was Vadim talking about?

I gasp and turn on my heel when I hear the lock turn.

The man with the bloody shirt stands in the doorway. He doesn't say a word. He only watches me silently. I consider running past him, but Vadim's words whisper in my ears.

"If you run, you will die."

Obviously, there isn't any talking sense into that psychopath, but what about this man?

Handsome, yes. He is darkly handsome, but is he sane? I highly doubt it.

I'm smart. I was a straight A student. I've made rational decisions my entire life thanks to my mother's guidance. What would she do? Would she run?

No. My mother never cowered in fear. She was the strongest person that I've ever known. She would have twisted this man's mind inside-out. He's some type of leader in all of this. It's him that I need to win. Not Vadim. Not the others.

Vadim said that this man decided to keep me. Why? Well, I'm not stupid. I know I'm here for one thing. To please him.

Placing both hands on the window sill behind me, I awkwardly stick my chest out and force a sweet smile across my face.

He tilts his head slightly as he watches me. He's intrigued. This is good.

I take a deep breath before pushing off of the window sill and taking a step forward. "H–hi," I whisper as I fiddle with my fingers nervously in front of me. Every ounce of resolve that I'd built up begins to drain away as he drinks me in with his cognac colored eyes. They trace every single inch of my body.

I had concocted an entire speech. I'd beg for my release. I would leave and never tell a soul, but when he begins stalking towards me, I have no words … I have not a single rational thought traveling through my head right now. I know only him in this moment. His presence within the walls of this room is impenetrable.

He's somehow cloaked my decidedness without a single word.

He stands merely inches away as I stare at his chest. My eyes trace each bloodstain before they travel to his mysterious eyes. His impassive state is bulletproof. There isn't any fooling him. In fact, I somehow come to believe that by even attempting to fool this man, I'd become the fool.

My mouth falls open, allowing a gasp to escape my lips as he grasps my arms in his powerful hands. Goosebumps spread across my body. Not from the cold, but from his touch.

"I … please," I breathe out.

Leaning down, he brushes his nose against mine. My head falls back as his breath spreads over my lips.

Placing his hand over the small of my back, he pulls me to him as his free hand tangles in my hair.

"Let me go," I rasp as my eyes roll to the back of my head.

The sensation is overwhelming. If he can do this to me with an embrace alone, what could he do otherwise? I feel so dirty and depraved for feeling this way, but I can't focus. Not now.

“I will not,” he says simply as he massages the back of my scalp. His fingers dig into my back as he holds me against him possessively.

“Why?”

I can’t pull my eyes from his as he whispers, “Because I saw you.”

Then his lips find mine, and I don’t stop him. I don’t stop him when he parts my lips with his tongue, and I don’t stop him when his tongue tangles with mine.

I don’t stop him because I want him.

My hands hesitantly creep up his muscular arms. I feel his power beneath my fingers as I grasp his broad shoulders.

He leads us to the bed before he pulls away and grasps my waist. The bed is soft beneath me as my back hits the mattress. He crawls over me before looking down at me.

“Do you know how to please a man?”

I frown as the tears blur my vision. No. No I do not, and suddenly I realize that I can’t do this. I *shouldn’t* be doing this. I should be in America with Mirna ... safe in my home ... away from the men with guns.

"No," I squeak out as a tear escapes my eye. "Look, I'm not even American. I mean, I am, but my parents were both Russian. If you want an American, I'm not it."

A dark smile creeps across his face. "I want *you*. I don't want anything else."

I frown. "V–Vadim said that he had to find another American doll…. Please," I whisper as I sit up on my elbows, allowing the tears that have collected in my eyes to freefall. "He killed my uncle and then he threw me in a cage … I just want to go home. You're different. I can tell."

I gasp when his hand wraps around my throat before he slams my head onto the mattress. He smiles deviously as my bottom lip begins to tremble.

Leaning down, his rough cheek brushes against mine as he whispers into my ear, "Do yourself a favor and realize that I am no different than any of the other men who occupy my family's dacha." He pauses momentarily as he inhales the scent of my hair. "If anything, I am much worse."

My lips part as I exhale a shaky breath. "Are you going to kill me?"

His grip loosens around my neck as he narrows his eyes at me. "You ask that now because you are afraid of death. I'm afraid that will soon change. One day, very soon, you will beg. You will throw yourself at my feet, and you will plead for me to end your life."

My hands wrap around my throat frantically when he slips from the bed and stands. He approaches the window, and I watch as he pulls his shirt over his head as he looks out.

My eyes travel over his muscular back as the words sit on the tip of my tongue. I lay frozen on the bed where he left me. What he has in store for me, it can't be good. My gut tells me that he wasn't lying when he said that he was worse, but how much worse? What does he intend on doing to me?

"What's your name?" I whisper as I look at the hardened expression on his face as he looks out the window.

He turns slightly, the flames of the fire cause his shadow to grow behind him. "My name is Dimitri. Welcome to my home."

Chapter 8

Little American Dolls

VADIM

The clicking from the 8MM camera reverberates throughout the room as I stand back and watch Vlad—who we lovingly call Vlad the Impaler.

He's prepping the brunette girl. Her head sways from side to side in her drugged state as he spreads her legs open wide for the camera.

This client specifically asked for a brunette between eighteen and nineteen years old. Big tits: check. Small waist: check. Lush lips: check. Pretty face: check.

I left the small village in which I was raised to come here and work for my uncle and cousin. Mama and Papa were not happy one bit. Papa escaped the family as soon as he was old enough. Dimitri's father, though, he understood our destiny. He understood the need to continue our legacy.

I had to seek them out when I began hearing the stories. I knew that this was my destiny, too. To keep our tradition alive.

Though, I'll never bequest the leading position of this Bratva—that goes to Dimitri.

Unless he dies first.

The thought of killing one of my own is bloodcurdling, however, the thought of my unstable cousin being the leading man makes my blood run hot. He doesn't have his head on right. He never has, and my uncle knows that. We all know that. But, tradition is tradition. I've just got to keep him in line now, and when that time comes .... I'll be damned if I allow our empire to fall because of his stupid decisions, like deciding to keep the blonde American as a living sex doll.

He was out of line in doing that, and Dyadya Albert will be none too pleased when he discovers what his dear son has done. It's a shame that it will be another couple of months before he returns to this dacha. He's in Saint Petersburg living a life of luxury with his young wife while we do all of the hard work. This place was originally a seasonal home and has been in our family for generations.

“Let’s move this along,” I snap as Vlad runs his fingers through the girl’s hair.

He stops abruptly and nods. I can’t see his expression through the gimp mask that he wears, but I’m sure he’s sneering. It’s imperative that he hides his face. Nobody can trace these tapes, hence why we use the 8MM camera. The tapes that we produce and distribute are meant for one person and one person only.

The people who purchase them from us buy them for hundreds of thousands, and sometimes millions. What a person will pay to have a person fucked, tortured, and killed in their name surprised me at first. It doesn’t anymore. After two decades of helping produce these films, it’s hard to shock me anymore.

Vlad looks toward me and I nod for him to begin.

This client payed a pretty penny for this tape. A sick bastard he must be with some of the requests that he had. We never outright hand these tapes to the buyers, and we never meet them in person. These tapes travel down a long chain of porno dealers and traders before they land in their owner’s hands.

I reach into my pocket and retrieve the vial of white dust. I unscrew the lid before retrieving a bump with my pinky nail. I snort it up my nose as I watch Vlad approach the brunette with a spike studded dildo.

He strikes her across the face with it and she gasps as the blood trickles from the wounds onto her chest. They never scream at first because the drugs are so strong, but eventually she'll manage to wrap her head around what's going on. That's when they try to fight, but at that point they are too far gone … too wounded and weak from the loss of blood.

Money talks, especially in Russia. It manipulates you. It *changes* you. I would never in a million years do this without the money. I still cringe occasionally while I watch either Vlad or Andrei perform … and Dimitri. The killing isn't his job, but when the stresses of life creep up on him, he takes the victims on himself.

He loves cat and mouse, a game that he sometimes plays. Although those games are not filmed behind an 8MM. No. They are filmed and livestreamed on the dark web where people pay in bit coins, an online currency not meant to be tracked. The cameras used for cat and mouse are mounted throughout the maze that we built. Sometimes it lasts for minutes, and sometimes hours.

The mouse *never* wins.

I light a cigarette as Vlad continues to maul the woman. Her face is unrecognizable as he continues to hit her with the dildo before he shoves it up her cunt. And now, she screams.

It took her long enough.

He grasps her hair and whispers something into her ear as he continues to pump it inside of her. When he pulls it out, blood pours from the abused orifice.

"Toropit'sya!" I snap, telling him to hurry along. I'm fucking exhausted, and unlike Vlad, I'm not getting my rocks off right now.

He huffs and releases her hair abruptly before leaning down and retrieving a saw from beside the bed where she lies.

I look at my watch impatiently as he positions the saw right above the elbow of her left arm. She squirms slightly as he prepares to cut into her.

Finally, once all of her limbs and head have been detached, he's done. She is no longer one piece, but six. I shut off the camera as Vlad approaches me. Removing the gimp mask, his dark eyes find mine. The man is a giant. He stands over six-foot-five and his face resembles a bulldog.

"Next," he says, his deep voice booming.

I shake my head. "Not today."

He tilts his head as he glares at me. "The American doll?"

Throwing my cigarette onto the floor, I snuff it out with my shoe before turning and walking toward the door. "Not today."

I stand outside of the door and run my hand over my face as I stare at Dyadya Albert's portrait. The spotlight shines down on his sharp features. His brown eyes look hauntingly real as I stare up at him, imagining Dimitri's portrait taking his place once he becomes Pakhan—the boss—and Dyadya Albert's will be bumped to the next place. Yes, my cousin who is fifteen years my junior will be *my* boss. The thought makes me cringe.

I was named my uncle's Sovietnik, or counselor in other words. Dimitri should have been the one to be Dyadya Albert's most trusted, but obviously, he can't rely on a lunatic … on a fucking loose cannon. If it wasn't for Dyadya Albert's strong traditional beliefs, I'd be the next in line. He knows that I'd be a good Pakhan.

Shaking my head, I light a cigarette and begin walking down the hall, allowing my ancestor's eyes to watch my departure to my room.

Chapter 9

No Means Nothing in this Place

SOFIA

Dimitri went into the adjoining room, which I'm assuming is a bathroom. Judging by the sound of running water, I imagine he's showering.

I pace back and forth as I determine what to do next. He took the keys with him, so I can't get through the door, though I'm sure there is someone waiting beyond it to take me out if I even attempt to escape.

My eyes travel to a stand-up mirror across the way. Slowly walking towards it, I quickly glance around and listen intently to the running water.

I step closer as I look over my gaunt face. I would like to think that I was once a wholesome, fresh faced girl. Now, now I'm a girl who's seen the misfortunes of life. I miss Mama more than ever. She kept me safe. She only allowed me to see the good.

My brown eyes have dulled, and my sun kissed hair seemingly has too. If I were to guess, I've lost over twenty pounds since I've been imprisoned in this place.

I'll die here. I can either die fighting or die with my tail between my legs. I'd rather fight and lose the battle than to raise a white flag. I can't surrender to these men. I can't allow Dimitri to use me until I die from the inside-out.

I hear the water shut off and my heart is in my throat as my eyes frantically search for a blunt object of sorts.

I manage to locate what looks to be a paper weight on the desk. It's a pyramid shape and looks pure gold. I weigh it in my hand and determine that it's enough to break the glass.

As the bathroom door cracks open, I hurl the paperweight at the mirror, flinching as glass goes flying in every which direction. White dust creates a cloud around me, making me realize that what I thought was a paperweight was not; it was holding some type of powder.

One particularly jagged, pointed piece of glass slides right at my toes. Just when I bend down to retrieve it, strong arms encircle me.

I scream and manage to impale Dimitri's arm with the glass. It cuts into my palm as I force it further into his muscle. He doesn't do anything. He doesn't flinch, he doesn't cry out; his grip only tightens around me, and I feel like my ribs will crack beneath his hold.

My hand falls away from the shard of glass as I try and pry his arm off of me. He grips my hair and yanks my head back before growling in my ear, "Yavlyayetsya to, chto vse u vas?"

My neck hurts from how he has my head angled. A shaky breath escapes me as I try to find his eyes, but I can't as he holds me against his hard chest. The wetness from his naked body soaks into the silk robe as he breathes against my neck. My eyes travel down to his arm which is steadily pumping blood as the shard sticks out, probably keeping most of it in. He's wounded badly, but he isn't backing down.

"Yavlyayetsya to, chto vse u vas?" He yells it this time, causing me to flinch.

I shake my head as much as I can with my hair being in his vice grip. "I–I don't understand."

He snickers. "You are Russian, yes?"

I blink rapidly. "I don't speak Russian. I only know a little bit … not a lot. Please, I'm sorry. Don't hurt me."

He yanks my head back further, and I feel like my neck will snap in half at this point.

"I said … *is that all you've got*? You've already smashed the mirror that has been in my family for generations."

He yanks my head forward and my eyes lock onto our broken reflection. His eyes look black at this point. He looks epically *pissed*. He pushes my head down, forcing me to look at the broken shards on the floor. They're coated in the white powder.

"You've already spilled my coke all over the floor," he snaps before pulling my head back once more. I feel his rough, stubbly cheek against mine as his chest rises and falls against my back.

"I–I'm sorry," I plead as the tears pour from my eyes. "Please don't hurt me, I'm so s–sorry."

His chest rumbles against my back as he chuckles darkly. "You're sorry? *Sorry*," he mocks.

He turns me around abruptly before shoving me away, and I watch in horror as he plucks the shard from his arm, causing more blood to ooze out.

"You have pissed off a very dangerous man, little mouse. How will you ever repay me?"

I sob as he begins stalking toward me. A piece of glass nearly punctures my foot as I back away, almost causing me to lose my footing. I feel like the walls are closing in on me as he gets closer and closer, still clutching the glass shard in his hand.

He's got a towel wrapped around his waist, and for a moment my eyes actually travel down his sinewy body before my gaze locks onto his again.

His hooded eyes are intimidating. He looks at me as though he could ravage me … like he could rip me into tiny pieces before putting me back together and doing it all over again.

My back hits the desk that I was admiring earlier as his chest crushes into me. He still holds the shard and I wonder where he will stick it. Will it be my heart? My neck? My stomach?

"Open the drawer," he growls, causing my eyes to grow wider.

I nod hesitantly as my hand blindly locates the drawer. I'm afraid to take my eyes off of him.

"The gauze," he demands.

"Okay," I whisper as I pry my eyes from his and locate the roll of gauze.

He steps back and holds his wounded arm in front of him. He's bleeding a lot. I'm surprised that he hasn't passed out.

"There is a spray in there that will stop the blood."

I nod once more as I rummage through the drawer. When I believe that I've located the spray, I hold it out in front of me with my trembling hand. He nods, confirming that I've found it.

"There is antiseptic in there, as well as tape. Get them out."

Once I've retrieved all of the items, I look up into his angry eyes.

"Clean it," he demands.

I do the best that I can with trembling hands, first pouring the antiseptic over the wound before spritzing the spray onto it. Then I wrap the gauze several times around his forearm, watching as the blood bleeds through. The spray worked for the most part, but he's still bleeding slightly.

My gaze moves from his dagger eyes to the shard that he still clutches with his bleeding hand.

"Turn around," he rasps, and I freeze. He's going to slit my throat.

I shake my head emphatically as I place my hands over my neck. "Please—"

"Turn. Around," he grits out, and I squeeze my eyes shut as I follow his order.

He grasps my wrist suddenly before slamming my hand onto the surface of the desk.

"I think we should start over. Hello, my name is Dimitri."

I swallow hard as I stare at my hand. What is he getting at?

"I'm Sofia," I murmur through trembling lips.

He inhales my hair before running his nose along my neck. "Ah, Sofia. Such a beautiful name for such a pretty girl. Let's get to know each other, *Sofia*. First, I'd like to start with a game. How does that sound?"

My body is shaking profusely. I can't will myself to respond. I have no words, and my body seems to be frozen in place as I stare down at my digits.

"Yes," he continues, "It's a game that my cousin's and I would play when we were younger. You may want to spread your fingers a little farther apart than that, though. The game is a little risky, but I'm very good at it. Well, I'm good when I play it how it's supposed to be played—with my own hand. I think yours will do just fine, though."

I begin sobbing uncontrollably when he places the hand with the glass shard next to my spread fingers.

"Shhh," he whispers against my neck. "You'll want to be very still. Trust me, little mouse." He pauses before kissing my neck. "Trust me."

He holds the shard over my fingers and I squeeze my eyes shut as he begins singing.

"The beauty of my fingers, is at risk tonight..."

With each word I can feel the shard hit the space between each of my fingers.

"As we sit here together, and play with this sharp knife..."

I force my eyes open and watch anxiously as the glass moves quickly between my fingers, and the pace continues to quicken with each lyric. The wound from his hand leaves trickles of blood on top of my hand.

"Stab, stab, stab, stab, stab, stab.

And hope that we don't slice,

The skin upon our fingers,

And dare to not get diced!

Stab, stab, stab, stab, stab, stab.

The blade is moving fast!

And if you're very lucky,

Your fingers they will last!"

I scream and nearly fall back when he impales the desk with the glass shard and backs away. His arms wrap around me once more as he runs his hand over my hair.

"See? I'm pretty good, yes?"

"Let me go!" I cry out. My chest vibrates with each sob that escapes me.

He kisses my cheek before turning me around in his arms. "Are you saying that you want me to put you in the cage again? I'd hate to do it, Sofia. You'll die down there, but if it's your wish …."

"No!" I exclaim, placing my hands on his chest. "I can't go back down there … I … I can't …."

I still haven't allowed my mind to linger on the thought of what could have happened to the young boy when Vadim unapologetically pulled him from the tiny cage. For my own sanity, I block the suspicions from invading my thoughts. Whatever happened to the boy, it couldn't have been good. Whatever happened to him was likely *horrific*.

He smiles and I flinch as he runs his fingers over my cheek. "I knew you cared. You and me … we can have a great life together."

I run my hands over my eyes, wiping away the tears. When I thought that he wasn't sane earlier, that was an understatement. He's fucking delusional to boot.

"I want you, Sofia. Tonight. In my bed."

I shake my head. "I can't … please."

He frowns and pouts mockingly. "No? I was wrong about you? This is such a disappointment, Sofia!"

I flinch as he throws his hands up. "First, I save you from the torture that would have occurred below. Then, I take it easy on you when you destroyed my family's things!" He places his hand over his heart as he plays up his exasperated state. "I'll go and fetch Vadim, I'm sure Vlad is ready for you."

I step toward him and grasp his arm gently. Looking up at him through bleary eyes, I'm realizing that he won't budge on this matter. If it was only him here, it would be one thing. But it's not. These men won't hesitate to kill me. Dimitri is the only one that's safe so long as I can keep him happy.

Licking my lips, I try and force the words past them. I'm caving in. I'm trading my pride for survival, and I'm afraid that's the most sickening feeling of all. If I were home, there would be search parties looking for me. I'd probably be rescued by now. But that isn't the case. I'm so far away from refuge. I must survive, and the only way that I can do that is by surrendering my heart, my body, and my soul.

"I'll stay with you," I whisper, my tone wavering as I surrender my dignity.

He smiles knowingly as he wraps his arms around my shoulders before kissing the top of my head. I rest my cheek on his chest and listen to his steady heartbeat as he runs his hands down my back to the curve of my ass.

"A man like me must have what he wants, Sofia," he murmurs as he reaches in front of me and pulls at the belt of my robe. I have nothing underneath and my body begins shaking as he slowly opens the robe to display my naked form beneath.

"Relax," he breathes out, and I listen.

I sigh as he cups my breasts in his hands before gently squeezing. His mouth crashes into mine, and he doesn't hesitate to slip his tongue past my lips as his fingers tangle in my hair. It almost seems like we're floating across the floor as he leads me to the bed.

When the back of my legs hit the bed, he pushes the robe over my shoulders before lifting me up and placing me onto the soft bedding. His hard chest presses into mine as he puts the majority of his weight on his elbows. His abstruse eyes lock onto mine, seemingly seeing into my very soul. He tells me with a look alone everything that I need to know. *Freedom* is nonexistent for me. I've garnered his attention, and he doesn't plan on giving me up anytime soon.

"Open up for me, little mouse," he whispers, his tone gravelly and full of need.

A single tear rolls over my cheek as I open my shaking legs. My muscles scream in resistance as he rests his hips between my thighs. I know nothing about this man, yet he is taking something so precious to me. Something that I never intended on giving to anyone until I was absolutely sure.

The realization bubbles beneath the surface as I try to keep my mind. He's going to rape me. This is rape. I was given an ultimatum. I either let him have me, or I would die. There wasn't an option.

My breath hitches as I reach up and place my hands on each side of his face. "If I do this … will you hurt me? Will you … will you let *them* hurt me?"

He smiles deviously as he places his hands over each of my cheeks, circling my skin with his thumbs. "Little mouse, I won't let anyone hurt you. I can't say the same for myself, because I'm sure …." He pauses as he slides a hand down my stomach to my opening.

I gasp as he runs a finger through my folds. I'm embarrassed by the evident desire between my thighs as he continues. "I'm sure you will require punishment from time to time."

He slams a finger into my opening and I cry out as I grasp his shoulders.

"And when you do require punishment, Sofia, you must remember that it's for your own good. I chose you. Only you," he rasps as his finger continues to move in and out.

He pulls out of me and holds his bloody finger in front of him, a wicked smile covering his face. "And it looks like you chose *me,* too."

My body seizes up when he reaches down once more, this time lining himself up at my entrance. I hold my breath as he enters me, stretching me more and more. White hot pain travels throughout my body as my head rolls to the side. Squeezing my eyes shut, I try to go to a happy place, but he doesn't allow that.

He grasps my jaw and pulls my face forward. "Open your eyes, little mouse. Show me your admiration. Show me those beautiful eyes that beg so well. Show me."

My eyes spring open, allowing the tears that have collected to escape.

"There," he whispers as he slowly begins moving in and out. "You're so beautiful … and you are *mine*."

Chapter 10

Love of my Life, Do Not Escape Me or You Will Die

DIMITRI

I take a swig from the bottle of vodka as I run my hand over the tacky wallpaper in the hall. Stopping at my father's portrait, I sneer.

"Chertovski mudak," I murmur before taking another gulp of the bottle's contents. Soon, that will be me in his place. Soon, I will turn this place upside-down with remodeling. *Soon* couldn't be soon enough. I fucking hate being under his tyrannical rule.

"Dimitri, you must be a role model."

"Dimitri, you must stop drinking and snorting coke up your nose."

"Dimitri, sometimes I think that you are no son of mine."

No, he's a bastard and I can't stand him. I can't stand that little weasel, Vadim, either. How am I expected to rule this Bratva when my own father cannot trust me as his council? He put Vadim in the position that was rightfully mine. And to think, I am to listen to Vadim until I am old enough to *"make wise choices."* I will never, ever allow him to rule me. Once my father dies, the throne will be mine, and I have every intention of leading this Bratva with an iron fist.

I snicker as I continue down the hall, running my hand over each portrait causing them to tilt. It will amuse me when Vadim frantically straightens each one.

I cannot wait for the day when I sit in the same chair that my ancestors sat in as an artist paints my features. My father is old, pushing his mid-seventies, so it's not much longer until that time comes.

The Vavilov Bratva has been in operation for decades. The government was vulnerable after the fall of the Soviet Union, so we took that as our chance to grow. We deal in human trafficking, drug trafficking, organ trade, and pornography—though, we only began producing and distributing snuff films about twenty years ago. That is our moneymaker. That's what sets us apart from the other bratvas.

I am the only son of Albert Vavilov. My sister, Alina, has nothing to do with the bratva. Women are not allowed, though she doesn't hide her love for the extravagant life that she lives as a result of our profitable business. She's a successful model. Beautiful, yes, but incapable of love, so she isn't much different than the rest of us. The Vavilov's are a cold, heartless breed.

I stop outside of the door as I listen intently to the others as they drink.

The door is opened enough for me to hear their antics before I kick it open the rest of the way. They all look up at me eagerly. The fear in their eyes always makes me smile.

"Brat'ya!" I say, spreading my arms out.

I place a hand over my heart. "I am in love!" I say with the most saccharine tone.

They laugh as I enter the room. Placing my finger beneath my nose, I inhale her sweet scent that still lingers. I can see the blood from her innocence beneath my fingernails as I circle around, placing my finger under each of their noses so they can smell my victory.

Vlad huffs as I plop down in my arm chair.

"I had only two kills tonight, and I had no fun killing off the boy," he says before taking a gulp of his beer. "The American would have eased me into a deep sleep tonight."

My face falls into a frown as I eyeball him. "Well, that is too bad then, isn't it?"

He sneers at me before averting his eyes.

"And where is Vadim?" I ask before taking another swig of the vodka.

Vlad's eyes travel over my shoulder. I look behind me and smirk when I see Vadim standing there watching me. I stand and whip around to face him, holding the bottle in front of me. "Cousin! So nice of you to join us!"

He sneers at me before snatching the bottle from my hand and taking a swig. Shoving it back towards me, he falls back onto the leather couch. "Did you kill her yet?"

I laugh. "Kill her? Of course not. I am in love."

He scoffs at my declaration as I take a seat on my arm chair once more.

"You know nothing of love, cousin." He snorts.

My jaw tightens. The need to break this bottle and saw his fucking head off makes my fingers tighten around the glass. "And you do, *cousin*?" I retort, fully aware that I'm pushing the only button that he has.

I watch as his jaw tenses and it makes me smile. He would kill me if he could. The feeling is mutual.

He reaches into his pocket, retrieving a folded piece of paper before sliding it across the coffee table.

I reach over and snatch it up before my gaze snaps to his. "What is this?"

He shrugs before running his hands down his face.

Smiling, I open the letter hastily, nearly ripping it in half. My eyes scan over the words. It's a letter from Sofia's mama, but that's not what shocks me. It's her mama's name that immediately catches my interest.

"It can't be," I murmur as my eyes flit to Vadim's and then back to the letter.

He reaches back and massages his neck as he slumps further into the chair. "I'm afraid so. She had it in her pocket when I took her. I only found it when I had her shower."

I leap up from my chair, causing the vodka to slosh from the opening of the bottle. "Do you know what this means?" I ask as my eyes grow wide.

He shakes his head slowly. "It means nothing until your father returns. Do not say a word to the girl."

I smirk as I turn, tucking the letter into my pocket.

"Dimitri!" he growls from behind me, and I stop in the doorway.

"Don't worry, cousin. I will not say a word," I say sardonically as I make my way back down the hallway.

“Man is not what he
thinks he is, he
is what he hides.”

-ANDRE MALRAUX

Chapter 11

One Family's Secret can be Another Family's Gain

VADIM

My mind is racing as I watch the brunette shlyukha circle the pole. Her movements are slow and mesmerizing as she works the stage. It's calming, even with the cocaine coursing through my veins.

If Dimitri utters a word to Sofia, so help me I will kill him myself. She should have stayed below, awaiting her time to go, but the fucking idiot had to decide to keep her. Though, this could play in our favor. Only time will tell. Dyadya Albert's reaction could either be good or bad. But how was I to know who the girl was? When I saw the letter, I knew that I had fucked up in taking her. I don't know half the people who live in that shithole village. I've never cared to know any of them.

"Drugoy napitok?" The waitress asks. She's pretty until she smiles.

I nod, slipping her 400 rubles. "Vodka."

Sinking further into the chair, I finish off my drink before lighting a cigarette. Perhaps it's a good thing that she's still alive.

We finally might get the leverage that we needed against our biggest rival.

I stumble out the door and wipe my arm over my mouth. My vision is blurry and my heart beats rapidly. I overdid it tonight. I need to have a clear mind, and the cocaine does that for me. However, mixing it with vodka never plays in my favor.

When I begin walking to my car, I spot a familiar face. I squint in her direction as I watch her bend down and talk to a potential customer.

"Fuck," I growl as I immediately march over to her and grasp her arm. The man at the wheel immediately takes off when he sees me.

"Galina!" I sneer as I back her into the wall outside of the strip club. "I thought you were done. You said after I gave you money the last time that you would get a job! You swore that you would stop this!"

She laughs as I look into her eyes. Her pupils are so dilated it hides the beautiful amber color.

Yanking her arm away, she turns and lights a cigarette.

"Galina, this has to stop," I rasp as the defeated feeling creeps up my spine. She just looks out into the congested street without acknowledging me.

"I demand that you stop this!" I exclaim as I narrow my eyes at her. She inhales another puff of smoke as she looks on.

"Galina!"

She whips around to face me and the light outside of the club shines down over her hardened features. She's changed so much. The drug abuse is evident as I look over every line in her face. Her lips have thinned and her eyes look sunken in. She's a mere shell of what she once was.

"You do not own me, Vadim," she snaps before throwing her cigarette down and snuffing it out with her high heel. "Not anymore."

I watch as she saunters away, her eyes scanning each vehicle carefully as she searches for her next client.

“Hey man, can I get one of those?” an American says as he gestures to the pack of cigarettes that peek out from my pocket. I roll my eyes before retrieving the pack and offering him a smoke. I light my own before lighting his as I continue to watch her walk away.

“Girlfriend problems? That’s a tough break,” the American says, attempting to make conversation. I turn and shove past him before murmuring, “She isn’t my girlfriend. She is my wife.”

Chapter 12

Home is no Longer where the Heart is

SOFIA

I want nothing more than to reverse the hands of time.

I would have saved my mother by not rushing her before Nationals. I just kept pushing and pushing her that night. The texts and the voicemails … tormenting her with guilt as she hurried to get to the ice arena to see me perform.

I would take back the accomplishment of winning first place and executing that triple jump effortlessly. I would take it all back if it meant that I could bring her back to life … to go home and see her burning something once more. She couldn't cook and she was rarely home on time, but that didn't matter. She was a remarkable mother and person. She would give her last penny to see me succeed and she would give anyone the shirt off her back.

When she died, my home was no longer. The vacancy was overwhelming, even with Mirna there. That alone was enough for me to reaffirm my reasons to come to Russia. Without mom, I was alone. Without mom, I had no home.

Now, I'm caught up in this mess, wrapped in the arms of a dangerous man … afraid to budge because of what he might do when he wakes.

It's not a good idea to wake a sleeping beast.

I didn't sleep at all last night, and I barely welcomed sleep when I was in the cage. My body and soul are spent. My mind is scattered as I watch the sun peek over the Caucasus Mountains in the distance. Now that it's light out, I can see the vast wilderness below, causing my heart to sink further into the pit of my stomach.

Dimitri must have partied hard last night after he left me naked, in a fetal position with the side of my face in a puddle of tears.

He wasn't gentle, leaving bite marks on my breasts and neck. My neck is sore from where he held me down against the bed, nearly making me lose consciousness several times. The most sickening part is the throbbing reminder between my thighs where he pumped into me feverishly, ignoring my cries for him to stop.

My eyes snap shut when I feel him stir behind me. He buries his nose in the crook of my neck as his arm tightens around my waist. I feel his length growing against my back as he rocks against me.

"Wake up, beautiful," he whispers against my neck, sending a chill down my spine.

I continue to pretend that I'm asleep until his hand slips between my thighs.

"Sofia," he breathes out as he begins to slowly circle my sore mound.

My eyes flutter open when he rolls me onto my back and stares down at me. "Did you sleep well, little mouse?"

I nod slightly without saying a word as he circles his index finger on my cheek. "I didn't think you could get any more beautiful, but this … it seems that I've woken to an angel in my bed."

I force a smile as he continues to play with me, causing the heat to build in my core. It makes me want to slap myself. He shouldn't be able to manipulate me this way.

He leans down before pressing his lips to mine. When he pulls away, a gasp escapes my lips as my core tightens.

“Come shower with me,” he murmurs, his breath blanketing my lips.

“Okay,” I whisper, willing myself not to cry. Though, I don’t think I can anymore after seven days in hell.

I stand nude in the bathroom as he starts the water. Steam quickly rises, covering us below our waists as he turns to face me. I cross my arms over my bruised bare chest as he takes several steps towards me. He grasps my forearms and pulls my arms away before he allows his hungry eyes to travel over my body.

His face turns dark as he narrows his eyes at me and releases my arms abruptly. “Don’t hide your body from me again,” he growls, causing me to flinch.

Grasping my arm tightly, he pulls me into the shower. His hard chest presses against my back as he wraps his arms around me and walks us toward the water. I welcome the warmth as the water pelts down over my head. My eyes flutter as he pulls my wet hair over my shoulder before planting light kisses along the crook of my neck. I feel a soft fabric run from my stomach to the valley of my breasts before he whispers for me to clean myself.

Grasping the washcloth from him, I begin to run it over my skin, feeling the burn from his hungry eyes.

When I bend down to wash my legs, he runs a finger down my spine, leaving tingles in its path. He gives me subtle touches, reminding me that he'll keep to his promise that I belong to *him*.

Once I finish, I allow the washcloth to fall to my feet as he ravages me. He kisses me along my side until he is kneeling behind me. He grasps my ass cheek in his strong hand before he sinks his teeth into the sensitive flesh, causing me to cry out. Grabbing my hips, he turns me swiftly. My back hits the black tiled wall as he lifts my legs, resting them over his shoulders before he buries his face between my thighs.

My mouth forms into an O as he assaults me with his talented tongue. My back arches as the unknown sensation creeps up on me. I have nothing else to grab, so my hands tangle in his dark hair as rivulets of water travel between my breasts and on to my stomach before landing on his tongue which laps at my sensitive nub viciously.

It's almost as if time stops as the orgasm sends a wave of fire throughout my body. My thighs squeeze his face as the ripples of ecstasy continue to send me higher as my core tightens more and more. A ragged breath escapes me as I come undone. I try to push him away as the feeling becomes overwhelming, but he won't stop.

"Please," I breathe out.

Finally, he releases me, nearly sending me crumpling to the floor as he stands. He reaches over me and shuts off the water before lifting me. I instinctively wrap my legs around his hips as he carries me from the bathroom to the bedroom. Once he sets me down, he immediately whips me around and shoves my face into the mattress.

He shoves into me with his length, leaving me dizzy as I grasp the soft sheets in my hands. His fingers dig into my hips as he once again sends me higher, this time from the full sensation that he gives me.

He's quick as he finds his release, and I panic when I think he's going to finish inside of me, but he quickly pulls out – spraying the warmth across my back as he growls. Leaving me halfway on the bed, I watch him as he approaches the wardrobe on the far side of the room.

"Go clean yourself off," he barks as he pulls his boxers over his hips. "Then come see what I got you."

I lift myself up with shaking arms before walking back to the bathroom. I use tissue to remove his come from my lower back before I peek out into the room. He's leaning against the wall as he eyes me.

"Come here," he murmurs, and his hooded eyes watch as I approach him.

He pushes off of the wall and smiles deviously as he places a white box on the chair next to him. "Open it. It's a gift."

I swallow hard as I approach the box before lifting the lid. I peer inside and see a pair of black stilettos sitting on top of a deep red cashmere dress. I pick up one of the shoes and my lips actually curl up slightly. I'm an athlete, and I've only worn heels on very few occasions. Where I can be graceful on the ice, I'm the opposite in a pair of heels. He wants me to wear this fancy stuff, and I want to laugh.

"Do you like them?" he asks, his voice gravelly, and my eyes travel to his own attire.

He's wearing a black leather jacket with a simple shirt beneath, along with some jeans and boots. He can wear streetwear, but I'm to wear something that looks as if I'm to attend an extravagant event. This entire thing is bizarre.

I force a smile and nod. "I love them. Thank you."

He returns the smile as he nods to the box. "Go on and put them on. I'm not done giving you your gifts, little mouse."

My smile drops into a frown as my shaky hands reach for the dress. Upon pulling it over my hips, I realize that it fits like a glove. Dimitri steps behind me and zips the back of the dress before kneeling down and slipping my feet into each of the stilettos.

My legs wobble as I attempt to stand upright. He smiles as he places his hands on my shoulders. He almost stands a foot taller than me, even in these God awful heels. He plants a soft kiss on my neck and it makes me want to fall apart. He isn't a gentle man, so his sensual side is confusing at best. I want so badly to find comfort somewhere, and when he touches me this way, I want it to be him. I know that can never be, though, after everything that he's done. Comfort would be having a choice, not being raped and then showered with gifts. If anything, gifting me these items helps ease his conscience, not mine. As do the tender touches. He's conditioning me.

He steps toward the accent table and retrieves a smaller box. Stepping in front of me, he opens it slowly, exposing my eyes to the many twinkling diamonds which lie inside. My gaze travels over the precious stones before my eyes find his. He smiles smugly as he walks around me.

I lift my hair as he slides the extraordinary necklace around my neck. The necklace is heavy, almost dipping between my breasts as he secures it at the nape of my neck.

"This necklace is worth almost two million dollars in the United States. I paid many rubles for this piece, and I will continue to buy only the very best for you, Sofia. *If* you continue to please me."

He walks over to the table and my eyes land on two more boxes. "I will leave you alone so you can prepare for our family breakfast. Make it quick. It starts shortly."

He turns and swiftly leaves the room. I walk to the table and open the boxes. One is full of high-end makeup and the other with extravagant hair pins, perfumes and toiletries. I can't understand what any of the items are, other than the obvious ones of course.

I carry the boxes to the bathroom and begin preparing myself for the *family* breakfast.

Dimitri returns just as I'm putting the last bobby pin in my hair, securing the chignon at the side of my head. My long bangs scoop down nearly hiding my left eye as Dimitri's reflection appears behind mine.

"You look stunning," he rasps as he approaches me and buries his face in my neck. "If I could have you right now, I would. Speaking of, you have an appointment this afternoon."

I frown. "Appointment?"

"Yes," he responds. "With your vrach."

I tilt my head, surprised that this is one of the few Russian words that I actually know. Then again, my own mother was a doctor.

"Doctor?"

He nips at my neck as his cognac eyes travel to mine in the reflection. "Yes. I do not wish to impregnate you—at least not yet."

My eyes grow wide causing him to laugh. "I would like to be as intimate as possible with you, and I can't do that when I can't come inside of your *cunt*."

The way he says the word causes me to noticeably cringe. He narrows his eyes at me before grasping my jaw and yanking my head back.

"That is no way to react, little mouse. You need to beware how you cross me. I will not hesitate to strike."

I suck in a breath as he abruptly releases me before grasping my arm.

He drags me down the hallway, and I try with all my might to stay on my feet.

Chapter 13

Russian Roulette

DIMITRI

Stopping right at the door of the breakfast area, I look down at Sofia. She is the perfect little showpiece in the dress that I bought her. Her breasts are nearly pouring from the fabric with each breath that she takes. Her lips are red and her brown eyes are sad.

I run my fingers over the many diamonds surrounding her neck. Her eyes flutter as a sigh escapes her lips.

"Are you ready to meet my family, little mouse?"

She exhales shakily as her glimmering eyes find mine. "You'll keep me safe?" she whispers.

Smiling, I place a hand over her cheek causing her to flinch slightly. "Nobody is to hurt you, Sofia. No one but me."

Sofia blinks several times before her eyes snap back to the double doors.

Placing my arm around her waist, I push the door open.

The commotion drowns out as wide eyes travel from Sofia to me. I smile smugly as we enter the room. "Brat'ya, Sofia will be joining us from here on out."

I pull out a chair for Sofia and she sits clumsily. She can't peel her eyes away from the dangerous men who surround her. They take her in with starving eyes, and she knows it.

I take my seat at the head of the table. Sofia sits beside me, right across from Vadim's soon to be occupied chair.

Reaching under the table, I grasp Sofia's leg tightly causing her to startle.

"I'm sure you are starving," I murmur as her eyes find me. She nods slowly before her gaze drops to her empty plate.

I smirk when I look towards Vlad's stone cold face. His eyes are locked on Sofia as he squeezes the fork in his large hand.

The door opens abruptly and Vadim saunters in. His eyes are on the floor as he hastily makes his way to his seat before plopping down.

"Cousin," I say sardonically. "So nice of you to join us. You had a rough night, yeah?"

He glares at me and I watch his gaze soften when his eyes land on Sofia before snapping back to mine as he shakes his head in disapproval. "I'll be alright."

The wait staff comes out and hands us each a menu. Sofia's eyes scan over the words. She can't understand them of course, because her idiot mother never taught her our native tongue.

I place my hand over hers and her eyes flit to mine. "I'll order for you."

She nods before placing the menu on top of her empty place.

"Brat'ya," I say, steepling my fingers as I look toward each of my men. "Sofia will be staying with us for some time. I'd like for each of us to help her learn her Russian roots. Starting with language, culture, and cuisine."

Vadim scoffs, "We all have jobs other than catering to your shlyukha."

A self-satisfied smile spreads across my face. “That is no way to treat our guest, Vadim.”

His eyes blaze as his jaw tenses. “Judging by the bruises all over her, I suppose that you are a shining example of how we are to treat our *guest*?”

My lips twitch into a smile as his eyes bore into mine. “What occurs between Sofia and I behind closed doors is nobody else’s concern.”

I grasp her small hand in mine and run a thumb over her knuckles. “Vadim, I would like if you would be her tutor. Teach her the language and the culture of Russia.”

He laughs. “Find somebody else. I have no time for it.”

“What would papa say, Vadim? I’m sure he would agree that we make her feel at home and teach her the ways of our country. Don’t you?”

He shifts in his chair as he diverts his eyes.

“Great,” I say as a member of the staff steps next to me with a pen and pad.

“Sirniki dlya menya, i blini dlya ledi,” I say as the woman scratches the order onto the pad before moving onto Vadim who waves her away.

I look toward Sofia. “I ordered you blini, it’s like a crepe. You *do* know what a crepe is?”

She nods, her eyes never leaving her plate.

I turn my attention back to Vadim. “I would like to begin assisting with the production of the videos. I’ve been wanting to do it for some time, but I could never find the motivation.” I pause as I look toward Sofia momentarily. “Now, I am very motivated. During that time, you can begin Sofia’s lessons. She is of Russian descent, so there is no reason for her not to understand our way of life.”

“Your father appointed me to this position for a reason, Dimitri. You do not give me orders.”

My fingers tighten around Sofia’s hand causing her to squirm uncomfortably in her chair.

The others around the table had gone on to converse amongst each other, but stop as they await my response to Vadim’s bold statement.

I glower at him. “Do not forget your place, Vadim. I am the next Pakhan, therefore you *are* to take orders from me.” I pause as I look toward Sofia with a slight smile. “You will begin working with Sofia this evening.”

My eyes snap to his as he balls his fists in front of him. His knuckles turn white as his face screws up. He'd be smart to shut his fucking mouth.

The food arrives and I release Sofia's hand as I look toward each of my men. "Let's eat. We've got work to do."

Vadim glares at me momentarily before his chair scrapes against the floor. He leaves the room hurriedly and I smile.

He needs to learn his place.

Chapter 14

Needing a Friend

SOFIA

It has been a busy day. After breakfast, a woman came into Dimitri's room pushing a rack of clothes with her. She mixed and matched blouses with skirts and pants, showing me the current fashion trends in Russia. She left the clothes here, and I assume that they're now mine to wear as I please.

If Dimitri weren't watching my every move, I would have grabbed her shoulders and shook her. I would have pleaded for her to help me.

I tried to tell her with my eyes alone, but she only smiled at me.

I was happy to change out of the dress that Dimitri had me wear and into some warm, fleece leggings. They're still stylish, and I matched them with a long crocheted sweater and ankle boots.

After the stylist left, the vrach came to me and gave me a shot for birth control. That's all she did. She didn't say a word. She simply stuck me in the arm and left.

I spent the rest of my day walking aimlessly through this massive mansion, discovering different rooms. One is full of taxidermy. I went to each of the poor animals, and as I looked into their marble eyes, I felt for them. Just like me, they're a showpiece … a prize. They were killed to be put on display, just like Dimitri is slowly killing me inside—only to dress me up like a doll and use me when he wants to.

Now, I'm waiting in the library as instructed. I stare out the window as my long hair hangs around my shoulders. I see a frozen lake outside and want more than anything to have the skates that my mother bought me. I would close my eyes and glide. I'd forget that the world that surrounds me exists. Maybe, just maybe, the ice would crack open and suck me under. That would be the most blissful escape.

I hear a voice clearing and turn to see Vadim with his hands tucked in his pockets. I'm so angry with this man, but what can I do? What can I possibly say that would encompass how torn apart I am inside because of what he did? I can't. I tried fighting before and it didn't do any good. So, I force a smile. I actually smile at the man who killed Uncle Artur and took me—the man that fed me a bite of stale bread every day and sprayed me like I was a stray dog.

He frowns as he walks across the library and takes a seat on one of the leather armchairs. My eyes travel back to the window as we sit in silence.

Finally, after several minutes, he speaks. “Privet, menya zovut Vadim.”

My eyes travel to him. His fingers run along the arm of the chair as he stares down at his lap.

“I’m sorry?” I rasp, turning my body slightly so that I can face him.

I watch his lips curl up slightly as he repeats himself. “Privet, menya zovut Vadim … it means, ‘Hello, my name is Vadim.’ Now you try.”

I twist my fingers in my lap as I shift uncomfortably on the chair by the window. “Privet … menya zovut Sofia.”

His eyes drift to mine. “Kak dela?”

Blinking several times, my eyes travel up to the cathedral ceiling. I know what he said, and I know how I’ll respond. He said, "*How are you?"* and I respond honestly.

“Grustnyy,” I breathe out, allowing a tear to seep from my eye before quickly wiping it away.

Sad. Yes, that’s an understatement. I’m many things. *Lost, broken, afraid, angry …*

I hear him sigh and my eyes find his before my gaze drops to my lap. “May I ask you a question?” I murmur.

“You may, but I can’t guarantee that I’ll answer,” he responds.

Crossing my legs Indian style, I rest my hands on my knees. “How old is Dimitri?”

“He is twenty,” he replies, not missing a beat.

My eyes wander to his. “And you’re his cousin?”

He nods slowly. “I am.”

“Is he your boss?”

He scoffs as he entwines his fingers in his lap. “Not yet.”

“Who is?”

He shakes his head. “My uncle. Dimitri’s father.”

“What is this place?” I implore.

Vadim runs a large hand over his scruffy face. “You said *a* question, not many questions.”

I divert my eyes. “I’m sorry.”

“But if you must know,” he continues. “This is our family’s dacha. It’s also where we do business.”

“One more question?”

He nods irritably.

“What is your business?”

He laughs. “I’m afraid that would require multiple answers, and I only promised one more.”

My eyes snap to his. “Can you blame me for wanting to know?”

He shakes his head, avoiding my gaze. “No, I cannot. However, that will all come with time. Now, I have some questions for you.” He pauses as he leans forward and rests his elbows on his knees. “Who are your parents?”

My lips part momentarily, but snap shut. Why does he want to know anything about me? It isn’t as though he could hurt them. They’re both long gone.

“David and Lidiya Dmitriev. They were my parents. They’re both dead.”

“Is that right?” he murmurs, and I nod. “How old are you, Sofia?”

I blink several times before answering. “I’m seventeen. I’ll be eighteen in a few weeks.”

I look up at his thoughtful expression as he stares off into the distance. “You really have no idea who you are, do you?”

It seems as if his question was to remain unspoken as he seemingly shakes the thought away. “Let’s continue.”

I sink back into the chair as I watch him carefully. Who does he think I am? Surely he knows nothing about me or my parents … or does he?

Chapter 15

Blood Thirsty

DIMITRI

I smile as I watch Vlad and Andrei wheel in the contraption that I've been working on for some time.

Vadim appears beside me as they begin strapping the girl down to the chair.

"What in the hell is that?" he asks as they secure her arms to each of the arm rests before moving on to her ankles.

I smirk. "Do you like it? I've been working on it for weeks."

His eyebrows sit high on his forehead as Andrei plugs in the electrical cord. A bag is over the girl's head and she begins moaning. I nod for Vlad to shoot her with the adrenaline as the 8MM clicks on.

"Dimitri," Vadim warns.

I hold my hand up to silence him. "What is the point of making these films if they are not screaming? If they are mostly dead already? What is the point? Our clients pay many rubles to see bloodshed, why not give them more? Why not paint the walls in red?"

I pause as I turn to face him. "You wanted to be humane to an extent, and I simply do not wish to run things that way. I want to make them squirm. I want to see them beg. Our customers are no different."

"Dimitri," Vadim says as Vlad removes the bag from her head. "You need to reign yourself in a bit. We do this job because there are sick fucks out there willing to pay to see it. You seem to have become one of those sick fucks yourself."

I chuckle as the girl begins thrashing around in the chair. "Perhaps," I murmur. "But you're no better than me, cousin. Quit pretending to be a hero. You've overseen many deaths in this very room, and now you question my methods?"

"You're going off the deep end, Dimitri," he says, his voice melancholy as disappointment reflects in his eyes. "You are to be the next Pakhan. You need to start acting like it. Leave the killing to those who we hired to *kill*. Leave the production to *me*. Let my conscience be the one to suffer. Pay attention to your job: being our future leader."

I smile as I pull the black, lacquered plague doctor's mask over my face. "That's where you're wrong, Vadim. I have *no* conscience to suffer. A *good leader* is an expert in all aspects of his business."

Sauntering over to the girl, her screams are like music to my ears. I turn and look into the lens of the camera, and as I tilt my head slowly I hold the knife in front of the camera before turning to the girl.

She shakes her head emphatically as she begs in a different language. Leaning forward, I grip the arm rests as I prod her with the long nose of the mask. She presses the back of her head into the chair as she attempts to escape my touch, but she can't go anywhere. She's stuck, and unfortunately for her, I plan on using this session as an example of how these videos will be from here on out.

"Let's begin," I murmur as I stand straight.

I circle her as I let the knife lazily run over her collarbone to her shoulder. I place the knife under the strap of her bra before the sharp metal slices through the fabric effortlessly, then I move on to the other strap. I keep cutting through fabric until she is bare before the camera, her entire body is shaking from a mixture of fear and the cold. This room is the equivalent of a meat locker. The rest of the home depends on fire places and furnaces, in which this room has none.

Vadim watches me intently as I run the knife from the girl's cunt to her neck. Her face is soaked from her tears as her head thrashes from side to side.

Using the knife, I sweep her black hair over her shoulder before leaning down and whispering, "Your time has come."

The chair that she is strapped to is not your average piece of furniture. I had cut a passage down the center. Beneath the opening, there is a track that I've attached to a large table saw. I hold the control in my hand. With one push of a button, her body will be slowly sawed in half.

Vlad and Andrei stand on each side of me with their hands folded in front of them. The camera clicks on as the light flashes erratically. Upon pushing the button, my lips curl into a smile from behind the mask when the saw comes to life between her thighs.

The girl's wide gaze stares down at the spinning blade as it inches closer and closer to her cunt. A mixture of sobs and screams escape her as the saw nicks the hood of her clit, and then all I can here is bone crushing as the saw begins to slice through her.

Her eyes roll to the back of her head as she howls towards the ceiling. She continues to convulse as the blade works its way from her pelvic bone to her midsection. Once it begins slicing through her vital organs, blood trickles over her bottom lip.

Eventually, the convulsing becomes an occasional twitch as the blade moves through her chest, to her neck and then to her head. The three of us are sprayed with blood and brain matter as the blade reaches the end of the track. I hold my arms out and smile deviously as I watch the door slowly close behind Vadim.

I run the knife along the wall as I approach my room where Sofia waits.

Pushing the door open, her gaze slowly moves from the book in her lap and then to me. Her eyes widen as she scrambles from the bed to the furthest wall. Her chest rises and falls erratically as she looks at me.

"Little mouse," I whisper as I close the door behind me, turning the key in the lock. Her body noticeably trembles as I approach her. I didn't bother removing the mask or cleaning myself off before going to her.

She holds her hand up as I get closer. "Dimitri, what happened to you? Are–are you okay?"

I hold my hands out as I step in front of her. "I'm okay, little mouse, but are you? You seem frightened."

Her lips twitch into a smile, but it doesn't reach her frightened eyes as she shakes her head haltingly. "I just thought you were hurt, that's all."

She cringes as I grasp her arms with my bloody hands. "I'm going to go take a shower, then I'd like it if we could watch a movie tonight? Does that sound alright? Will you watch a movie with me, Sofia?"

The gulp is audible as she swallows hard before slowly nodding her head. "Of course."

I smile as I pull the mask over my head. "You are so beautiful." I run my fingers over her cheek as a shaky breath escapes her lips. "I want to show you my art. I want you to appreciate it as much as I do."

She licks her lips before forcing a smile. "I can't wait."

Chapter 16

Cat and Mouse

SOFIA

Dimitri has my arm in a vice grip as he pulls me down the hall. I'm only wearing the robe with nothing underneath as he leads me to our destination.

I can't imagine what this movie is that he wants to show me, but I'm sure it isn't your average film. My stomach lurches as I think of the blood that he was covered in when he came into the room earlier. I knew he wasn't hurt. He hurt *someone*. I have a sneaking suspicion that that is what I'm to watch. I'm going to witness him hurting, possibly killing someone. The sickest thing is, he calls it his *art*. Painting and writing and dancing—that is *art*. Killing certainly is *not*.

Once we enter the room, my skin crawls under the many gazes that fall on me. The room is full of Dimitri's men. Except for Vadim. For some reason, I'm wishing that he were here. Maybe he could keep me safe from all of this. I don't know why I feel that way, but when we were in the library earlier, his presence was certainly different than before. He almost seemed human.

Dimitri leads us to a large armchair where I'm pulled onto his lap. I avoid looking at the other men as I try and pull the robe as far down my legs as possible.

Dimitri snaps his fingers next to my ear causing me to jump. One of the men dims the light before turning on some type of projector.

The quality of the video is weathered. The video itself is either really old, or it was taped with an old camera. All I can hear is an eerie clicking sound. My eyes travel around the room in which the video was taken. There isn't anything other than an old mattress and cigarette butts on the floor. Several seconds tick by when I see two masked men situate a strange chair in the center of the room.

It reclines and has what looks to be a blade protruding from the center. Then, the masked men place a girl onto the chair before they begin strapping her down. She can't be much older than me. She only wears a bra and underwear, and she looks drugged as her head sags to the side.

This reminds me of the beginning of a horror film. I love horror films, but this is frightening, because I'm afraid that this isn't a fictional slasher film. This is horror in real life, and I'm stuck in the middle of it—I've been stuck in the middle of it for over a week.

"Watch," Dimitri breathes into my ear.

The bigger masked man pulls out a syringe before plucking her in the neck, and it immediately seems like realization washes over her as she begins writhing. Placing my hand over my mouth, I force myself to look on as Dimitri steps into the camera's view. I know it's him because of that mask, the one that he wore when he came into the room soaked in blood. Chills shoot down my spine as he looks into the camera and tilts his head before holding the knife in front of the camera lens.

I keep telling myself that this isn't real … because I want more than anything for this to be a gory film with incredible special effects. However, it is real. I know because of the unadulterated terror written on her face as he runs the knife along her collar bone. He cuts away the bits of clothing that she wears before she is left terrified and nude. When he holds up the remote and presses the button, her wide eyes watch in horror as the blade inches closer. I turn my face from the projection as tears stream from my eyes. I'm thankful that there isn't any sound. It's just clicking. *Click, click, click.* She's dying, yet her screams are not to be heard.

Dimitri grabs my jaw and pulls my face forward, but I keep my eyes closed.

"Open. Them," he grits out, and I shake my head as much as I can with my face in his grasp.

"Open!" He hollers, and my eyes snap open as the drill slowly works its way through her body.

I manage to squirm out of his lap and fall to my hip as I sob. The clicking stops and all is silent for a moment. Then, all I can hear is laughter as I try with all my might to keep the burning vomit from erupting from my throat. The men laugh in unison as I come undone. The reality sets in more than it ever has at this point. I just witnessed a murder … a *horrific* murder.

"Why?" I choke out as my gaze travels to Dimitri's smiling eyes.

His chest shakes several more times as he comes down from his fit of laughter. His face drops into a frown as he stares down at me.

"Why?" he asks sardonically, before drawing out the word. "*Why?* What must you know, little mouse? You could have asked a better question; don't you think? You already know the answer to your inquiry, do you not?"

I lift myself with shaking arms and legs until I'm standing. "No. I don't know. I don't know why anyone would do that."

He smiles as he stands. He is inches from me as I back away, but my back hits something hard. I try to step away but two large hands grasp my arms. The other men begin to stand and slowly surround me as my heart thunders away in my chest.

"I am not *anyone*, Sofia. Soon, I will be the Pakhan of this bratva. *Soon*, I will lead these men. The videos? I'm afraid that you will need to accustom yourself. They are not going anywhere. I *saved* you. I didn't save you so that you may look down on me. You are *mine*, therefore you must accept what *I* am."

I grit my teeth as I stare up at him. "You're a monster, and I will *never* accept it."

He sneers at me. "A monster? Little mouse, you haven't seen anything yet."

The man behind me releases my arms and my eyes travel for an escape. They stand shoulder to shoulder as I turn on my feet frantically. I attempt to squeeze between two of them, but they don't budge. Instead, they begin shoving me back and forth. I cry out as I'm shoved into their hard chests as they bound with laughter. Tears streak my face as I pound on chests, but it's no use.

They stop laughing when a bang sounds from the door. The crowd disperses leaving only Dimitri and I standing in the center of the room. Vadim stands in the doorway with a stern look on his face. Dimitri's smug smile never lets down as he stares down at me.

"That is enough!" Vadim barks at the men. They all sit down as Vadim stalks into the room. He narrows his eyes as he approaches Dimitri. "I've sent for your father's early return. He isn't happy."

Dimitri scoffs as he turns to face him. "You ran to *Dyadya Albert* because you couldn't keep the peace. There hasn't ever been an issue before. What's the difference now?"

Vadim's eyes soften as they flit to me, but they immediately harden when they land on Dimitri once more. "I think you *know* what the difference is, Dimitri."

I wring my hands in front of me nervously as I look from Dimitri to Vadim, and then to the open door. That could have been me in that video. It could still be me someday soon. I can't imagine the imminent fear that she felt when that blade came to life, or the pain she endured when it sawed through her body relentlessly.

My heart races when I think about running. I'm fast, but not quicker than a bullet. It's either that, or being raped again … even worse, killed—not just killed, but tortured.

He showed me that tape because he wants me to know what he's capable of. He wants me to know that he can end me without a second thought, without any repercussions.

So, I run. I run on a wing and a prayer. I run hoping that my mother will somehow reach down from the heavens and scoop me up to safety.

Once I escape the room, I turn momentarily to see Dimitri on my heels. I grab the door and swing it as his face with all my might. My heart beats abnormally fast when I hear him grunt behind the heavy wood.

My feet pound the floor as I search for the stairs. Once I find them, I grip the rail. Looking down, I see two men waiting by the double doors as they talk casually. I opt to search for another escape down a different hallway when Dimitri slides to a stop. My wide eyes lock onto his as he pulls a strange cat mask over his face. It's eerie and has realistic whiskers protruding from the cheeks. It doesn't cover his mouth, and I watch as his lips curl into a wicked smile.

"Go on, little mouse," he whispers as he takes two steps toward me. "*Run.*"

I turn and run with all my might through this maze of a home. I hear his feet hitting the floor behind me, and I don't have enough time to stop and check the doors throughout the hallways, though I'm not sure how intelligent it would be to trap myself inside of a room. I could possibly barricade myself inside, but he'd get to me eventually. What if I did actually make it outside? I wouldn't make it out there either.

He has me under his thumb, and I realize that I'm running just to run. There isn't any feasible reason for it, other than I'm fucking terrified. My will has been condensed to fight or flight—I'm running like a scared mouse trying to escape a much larger animal. *Cat* and *mouse.*

He's going to eat me alive. This is a game to him. He wants you to run. Well, fuck him.

I stop once I hit a dead end and whip around to face him. He skids to a stop and slowly removes the mask from his face before dropping it beside him on the floor.

His eyes survey my body and I quickly realize that the robe has opened slightly, revealing the inner curves of my breasts.

“Am I here to die?” I ask, summoning his eyes back to mine.

Dimitri stalks towards me, and I want to back away with everything in me, but I stand my ground. He wants to frighten me. He wants to intimidate me into submission. He wants to take away the life that I’ve worked so hard for. I won’t give that to him. He cannot bleed me dry of my determination. My resolve. I *will* get out of here.

When he grasps my jaw, I don’t take my eyes off of him. When he pulls my lips to his, neither one of us close our eyes. We gaze at each other with a promise; it’s either him or me. I’ve never thrown in the towel with anything in my life. I don’t plan on starting now. The only way to get to Dimitri is to make him trust me.

I reach up and run my fingers through his hair as I press my lips harder to his. He growls as his hands slide over my hips, beneath the robe, leaving a trail of fire in their path.

Gripping my hips, he backs me into the table at the end of the hall as he kisses me feverishly. My back hits the table and I gasp when he pulls his lips from mine before sweeping pictures and other breakables from the surface. Glass shatters and slides across the floor as he lifts me and plants me on the edge of the table. He frantically rips the robe open before leaning down and drawing my nipple into his mouth. He bites down, causing me to cry out before he moves to the other one.

I grab at the hem of his shirt and pull it over his head. Grabbing his hips, I lean down and run my tongue along his abs until I reach his nipple. He sighs as I circle my tongue around his nipple before trailing my tongue over his chest and to his neck. I bite down hard and he digs his fingers into my hips as he groans against my neck.

"Ya khochu tebya," he growls as his fingers move to the button of his jeans.

He said *'I want you,'* and I respond in the way that he would want me to in the throes of passion. "Yebat' menya, Dimitri." *Fuck me Dimitri.*

He grabs my face with one hand as he lines himself up at my entrance with the other. I cry out when he thrusts into me and my head rolls back as he continues to fuck me feverishly. I hold onto his shoulders as I tighten around his length, the orgasm coming quickly as he loses himself in this moment.

I'm sure his fingers are leaving bruises around my hips as he uses them for leverage. I can't deny my own enjoyment of this encounter as I hear my wetness each time he pulls out before re-entering me.

Something in me is changing. Unlike the other times, I'm just as much invested in this moment as he is. I'm enjoying it. I want it. It's escapism in its rawest form; allowing my tormenter to also be my lover.

The table that he has me on knocks against the wall loudly as he seeks his release. My fingers curl around the edge of the table as I convulse around him. His head falls back as he gives one last thrust. He lets out a guttural growl and I feel him pumping his release inside of me as I look over his shoulder through lust drunk eyes.

Dimitri's head falls forward before he rests his forehead in the crook of my neck as we both work to catch our breaths, and I watch as Vadim's shadow descends down the hall.

I gasp as Dimitri sinks his teeth into my neck. "To answer your question, little mouse," he whispers against my flesh. "You are not going anywhere as long as you continue to do *that*."

Two Weeks Later

As I look into the mirror, I'm realizing how different I look with my cat eye makeup and crimson lips. My hair looks classic in a wavy side bun and my breasts are pressed up, displaying my cleavage. I pull the formfitting, black silk dress up over my hips before zipping it up the side. Then I slip my feet into the red stilettos before turning the light off and exiting the bathroom. I stop when I reach the new stand-up mirror that replaced the one that I broke.

Today is my eighteenth birthday. This would have been my senior year in high school. This year, I would have been moved from the Junior category to the Young Adult category for competition. I would have absolutely killed it this year, and it would have been for mom. Instead, I'm here, struggling to breathe.

Many days I'll stare outside aimlessly, wishing for nothing more than to feel the ice beneath my feet once more. When I was living my dream, I felt like I was floating in the clouds. I was free, yet determined. I wanted to see how far I could go, and I wanted the world to watch. My name was to go down in history, I was sure of it.

I'm no longer free, but my determination has not dwindled. It's a burning ember in my soul that I will not allow to die.

My heels click against the wooden floors as I descend the hallway to my destination. It's the same time and place every day when I go to Vadim. Our conversations always begin on an awkward note, but then they flow casually. I've learned a lot about my birth country. From the cuisine to the fashion to the language; Vadim isn't a bad teacher. He isn't bad to look at either.

At first, he was intimidating. Now, I sense a sadness about him. It's only evident on occasion, and I have to look closely to see it. When his black eyes that normally carry a promise of harm soften to a lighter hue, they twinkle as memories flicker behind them. His shoulders will slump slightly in defeat, but then he snaps back to his normal hardened demeanor.

Upon entering the library, my eyes grow wide when he's already here. Usually, I'm the first to arrive and he's fashionably late.

He stands in the middle of the library with his hands behind his back. My face flushes when he drags his dark eyes along the curves of my body.

"You're early today," I murmur as I close the door behind me.

He smiles, but it doesn't reach his eyes. "Of course I am. It's a special day."

"Oh?"

He lets out a gritty laugh as he takes his hands from behind his back. He's holding a package, and I take a hesitant step towards him.

"What is that?"

"It's a gift. For your birthday."

I cock my head as I walk the rest of the way to him. "How did you know it was my birthday?"

His face drops into a frown. It seems that I've stolen his moment and, for some reason, I actually feel remorse. He's the only one that I can trust not to hurt me in this place. His position regarding me changed immensely once I emerged from the cage. He's as much as a friend as one could have in the bowels of hell.

I smile and reach out for the package. Taking it from him, I turn and sit in on the chair and my eyes find his as I slowly lift the lid. His eyes dance around anxiously as I lower my gaze.

Inside the box lies a pair of black figure skates. They're beautiful and their new smell drifts from the box to my nose. I purse my lips as I push my tears back.

"They're top of the market. I hope you like them," Vadim says quietly.

I place the lid over the box and stare at the wall blankly. "This is very nice, Vadim, but Dimitri would never allow me to skate. I'm not allowed outside."

"The skates were only part of the gift, krasavaya. I've spoken to Dimitri and he has no issues with you utilizing the lake outside as long as you are not alone."

"What?" I breathe out, my eyes finding his.

His lips curl up mischievously. "We could go tomorrow if you'd like."

I can't help the elated smile that covers my face. I didn't think I'd be skating anytime soon. Perhaps I was right about gaining Dimitri's trust; allowing him to have a piece of me for bits of freedom. I'll take whatever he gives me at this point because each tiny fragment that he gives me back will result in my ultimate desire: *true* freedom with no restraints … an escape.

"Today will be a busy day," Vadim says as he sits in his usual seat.

I walk to the chair across from him and also sit. "What's today?"

He rests his elbows on the armrests as he steeples his fingers in front of his lips. "Today, the Pakhan returns."

Chapter 17

Time is Dwindling

VADIM

I stand next to Dimitri by the stairs as I watch the double doors eagerly for Dyadya Albert's arrival. Dimitri smirks as he waits, fully knowing that he is the reason for my uncle's early return. My uncle only learned about Sofia when I requested his return. I can't risk Dimitri hurting her any further, or disclosing any more of our business practices. He's a damn fool, and if I can't reel him in, maybe his father can.

The doors swing open and I stand straighter as Dyadya Albert enters with Alina, Dimitri's sister, and Dina, my uncle's wife who is about thirty years his junior.

I nod as I approach them. "Dyadya Albert, I am so glad you're here." I pause and nod to the women. "Alina, Dina …."

Alina smiles at me smugly before brushing her shoulder against mine and sauntering to her brother. "You've been stirring the pot, I hear," she audibly whispers behind my back, and he laughs darkly in response.

Dina looks around the foyer as she slinks out of her coat. "It's always so stuffy in here," she whines as she shoves the fur coat into the maid's chest. "Vodka with a peel of lemon. I'll be in our room."

The maid scurries away to ready her drink as Dina ascends the stairs after lazily kissing Dimitri on the cheek. She's already drunk mid-afternoon, which is never surprising for Dina.

"Where is the girl?" my uncle asks as he looks up at me through droopy eyelids.

I turn and nod to Andrei to go fetch her before my eyes land on Dyadya Albert once more. He's aging quickly. His shoulders are hunched as his bony hand grips his cane and his face sags down in wrinkles. The man never smiles unless he's playing a game of Vint.

I turn when I hear the clicking of Sofia's heels against the wooden steps. She's still wearing the tight black dress from earlier. It was hard to take my eyes off of her then, but it's even harder now that her eyes remain downcast and the tops of her breasts ripple from her fluttering heart.

Alina looks towards her curiously as she reaches the last step. Dimitri holds out a hand and she hesitantly gives him hers before he leads her to his father.

Dyadya Albert reaches towards her and grasps her chin. He slowly tilts her head from one side to the other as his eyes examine her features. “What is your name?” he asks, finally releasing her.

Sofia’s eyes slowly travel to his. “Privet menya zovut Sofia Dmitriev,” she whispers, causing me to smile slightly.

She’s absolutely stunning and quick to learn. We can carry on much of our conversations in our native tongue, and the way the words roll from her lush lips make me want to have her to myself. However, the way Dimitri holds her possessively against him is a stark reminder of what will never be.

Dyadya Albert nods toward me, yet his eyes remain on her. “Meet me in my office.”

“Marry her?” Dimitri exclaims as he leaps from the chair across from Dyadya Albert’s desk. “Are you *insane*? I'm twenty years old. I didn't plan to marry for another twenty years!"

My uncle slams his fist down on the desk. "Son, you are going to learn quickly that the Pakhan is to make sacrifices. Sofia Dmitriev is an asset. When he discovers that we have her and she is wed, he will have to work with us."

He pauses as he shakily stands, using his cane for leverage. "Marry the girl. She's beautiful and timid, and when the time comes, give her babies. Sooner would be better than later."

Dimitri sucks his teeth at the mention of a family, and I press my knuckles to my pursed lips as their argument continues.

"*Children*? Papa, I was using her for a good fuck. Not to wed, and not to have children. Not to mention she is a *Dmitriev*. I am a Vavilov." His voice drips with disgust at the mention of her surname.

Dyadya leans on his cane for support as he slowly shakes his head in disapproval. "Yes, but do not forget, the Dmitriev family can either be our biggest ally … or our biggest enemy."

Dimitri scoffs before whipping around and exiting the office, slamming the door behind him.

My uncle's eyes travel to mine. "Time is dwindling. I do not have much longer on this earth. I need you to promise me that you will help him fulfill this family's legacy."

I nod haltingly. "Of course. You have my word."

He begins walking to the door, but stops momentarily. "Vadim, you are more of a son than I've ever had. As tradition has it, Dimitri is to be the next Pakhan." He pauses and his eyes travel to mine. "I know you would be a good leader."

I nod once more as he exits the room. If that was supposed to make me feel better, it didn't. My loyalty to my uncle is undeniable, however, I cannot say the same for my cousin. He is pure poison, and now Sofia is to be forced to marry him. He'll either kill *her*, or he'll kill her *soul*. That is for certain. The question is, which one will die first?

Chapter 18

A Ring Without a Promise

SOFIA

We each stand on opposite sides of the room. Dimitri is adjusting his bow tie as he stares into the stand-up mirror. I am standing right outside the bathroom door looking over my made-up face. I'm wearing a long, flowing white gown with a fur draped over my shoulders. We are to attend dinner with his family. Nervous is an understatement. When I'm in the room with all of them I feel as though I'm up against a rabid pack of wolves as they gnash their teeth at me.

Dimitri hasn't spoken a word to me all day. I can't say it hurts my feelings, but it makes me anxious. He's angry, I can see the fire dancing in his eyes each time he looks my way. I can't imagine what I've done wrong. Then again, he's a ticking time bomb waiting to blow.

What I've done wrong. The thought makes me scoff inwardly. It also makes me incredibly sad. Of course

I've done nothing wrong. I was *taken.* I was *imprisoned.* I was *raped.* Yet, here I am, wondering what *I've* done wrong.

"It's time," he snaps, yanking me from my thoughts. I nod and stare down at the floor as I follow behind him.

Get through tonight, Sofia. Then tomorrow, it's you and the ice.

The doors to the dining room open as we approach them, and my ears fill with the sounds of an otherwise normal family dinner. It makes my heart hurt when I remember the family that I lost … the *life* that I lost. I never had a large family, and if I did, I didn't know any of them. But I did have Mom and Mirna. They filled that void; the void that will now forever be empty.

Glasses clink together as they toast, and smiles surround the table, except for Vadim and Dimitri's father, the Pakhan. They pause once we enter the room, and the beautiful brunette that I saw earlier stands to greet us.

"Sofia," she says, her voice is sultry as she rounds the table and grasps my hands gently in hers. "We didn't have a chance to meet earlier. My name is Alina. I'm the daughter of the Pakhan and Dimitri's sister. Please, come sit."

Her kindness is a shock. She doesn't look like the friendly type. She's beautiful and thin with perfectly arched eyebrows and thick pursed lips. Her cognac eyes confirm what she said; she's basically a female version of Dimitri.

She leads me around the table and I sit beside her as Dimitri takes a seat across from me. The Pakhan sits at the head of the table and the woman, who I'm assuming is his wife, sits beside him across from Alina. The other men that I've seen here and there also surround the table, and Vadim sits beside Dimitri. They're all staring at me like I'm an alien. I suppose I am in this place.

The woman, who I'm assuming is the Pakhan's wife, gives me a slight, fake smile before she takes a sip of her drink.

"Sofia, tell us a little bit about yourself," Alina says, nudging me with her elbow.

My wide eyes travel around the table. "I … um…."

"Sofia is a very talented figure skater," Vadim answers for me. "She used to compete and I'm hoping that she can again someday very soon."

Dimitri scoffs as he rolls his eyes. Asshole. Nothing that he does surprises me.

"Really?" Alina says, exasperated. "How long have you been figure skating?"

I stare down at my empty plate. "Since I was a toddler. My–my mother bought my first pair of skates … I never stopped skating after that."

"Your mother, what was her name?" The Pakhan says, and my eyes snap to his.

"Lidiya Dmitriev."

He nods. "And your father?"

I frown. I can't for the life of me wrap my head around why they keep asking about my mother and father. "David Dmitriev. They're both *dead,*" I say, realizing my bitter tone.

"Oh?" he remarks. "And how did they die?"

I blink several times before diverting my eyes. "My father had a brain aneurysm when I was very small. My mother was struck by a car and killed."

My eyes dart up to Dimitri when I hear him laugh subtly. "I'm sorry, is something funny?"

He shakes his head with a priggish smile on his face. "Not at all."

“Did you attend his funeral?” the Pakhan asks nonchalantly. I feel the blood rise to my face and do everything that I can not to scowl at him.

“No. I didn’t. I was too young.” I respond sharply.

The Pakhan’s lips curl into a tight smile as he surveys me. “Well, we are happy to have you here at our dacha. I hope that you have been made to feel at home, seeing as this *is* your home now.”

The tears burn my eyes as he makes a mockery of my circumstances, and I startle when Alina wraps an arm around my shoulder. “You and I will have a lot of fun this summer. It may look like a tundra out there right now, but it’s breathtaking once the snow melts.”

I give her a slight nod as I ball my fists in my lap.

Conversation picks back up around the table as I remain silent. Food is served along with more alcohol. I can feel the dim room lighten up with each drink that the family has. Though, there are still dark clouds hanging over my head … and Dimitri’s.

Vadim remains stoic as he takes small sips of his vodka. His back is straight as his eyes survey the different faces at the table. When his gaze lands on mine, he tilts his head slightly and his hardened demeanor seems to thaw, at least a little. We stare at each other for several seconds before the Pakhan taps his fork against his glass.

He doesn't say a word. Instead, he nods toward Dimitri who looks none too pleased. Dimitri stands and walks around the table to where I'm sitting. Reaching into his pocket, he retrieves a tiny jewelry box and sets it in front of me.

"Open it," he whispers, and I take a deep, shaky breath to calm myself.

When I open the box, my breath catches in my throat. The diamond stares back at me in all of its glory as my heart palpitates. I try and wrap my head around this entire situation, but how can I? There's been so much that's happened in so little time and this is the last straw. He's not only insane, but an absolute lunatic if he thinks that I would *ever* marry him.

He reaches down and takes the ring from the box before holding it out. He waits for me to hold out my hand so that he can slip it onto my finger, but I keep my hands balled in my lap as I stare at the princess cut diamond ring like it's the plague. He quickly becomes frustrated, grabbing my wrist and yanking my hand towards him before shoving the ring onto my finger.

He grips the back of the chair and his breaths nip at my neck as he whispers, "Congratulations, little mouse.

You've graduated from being my *whore* to my future *wife*." He pauses as he squeezes my wrist painfully, and I close my eyes to keep the tears from seeping out. "This isn't a Russian custom. We do not do engagements, but me being the *gallant* man that I am, I decided to try and make this special for *you* … since you aren't a *true* Russian."

He releases my wrist abruptly and my eyes snap open, allowing a single tear to roll over my cheek. I hurriedly wipe it away and my eyes stay on my ring finger as my hand remains unmoving atop the table.

Everyone begins carrying on once more like nothing even happened while my world crashes down around me. Except for one person. His black eyes peer into mine from across the table, and they say everything that I've needed since my mother died.

I'm so, so sorry.

I flinch when Dimitri slams the door, once he and I enter the room. I'm yanked around by my arm to face him, and his eyes resemble *hell.* His cognac gaze has turned amber, and the tiny flecks of light are comparable to dancing flames as he shoots daggers at me.

“You embarrassed me, Sofia,” he growls as his fingers tighten around my arm.

I can barely breathe as I stare up at him with pleading eyes. “I–I’m sorry.”

He doesn’t say a word, and I watch as his jaw tenses. I can almost see his thoughts of wanting to harm me, and it makes my heart skip a beat.

“You are an ungrateful bitch!” he hollers, and before I can speak a word, his fist connects with my face. I cry out as he releases me and I crumble to the floor.

He fists my hair and yanks me up before the back of his hand lands across my unharmed cheek, and I feel like my jaw is going to pop beneath the impact as my mouth fills with the coppery taste of blood.

“You are *nothing* to me!” he shouts, releasing my hair and slamming the toe of his dress shoe into my stomach.

All of the air leaves me as I cradle my throbbing abdomen. I try and defend my body as he continues raining down the blows, but my armor is quickly crumbling as his rage engulfs me, leaving trails of bruises across my once unmarred flesh.

He once again tangles his fingers in my hair before ripping my body from the floor and throwing me across the room like my body weighs no more than a feather. Once my body connects with the hard floor, I convince myself that my bones and organs are loosely banging around beneath my skin. I feel like a sack of bricks as I attempt to lift myself on all fours. Dimitri stands several feet away as he stares down at me mockingly.

"Come here," he says soothingly.

His sudden change in tone is not lost on me as I attempt to lift myself up several times. Once I succeed, I inch one hand before the other as I begin crawling to him. Hand, knee, hand, knee … the journey of crawling several feet is the equivalent of swimming across the ocean, or so it seems. My body is heavy, and each mark that he left on me screams in resistance as I will my arms and legs to work. I don't want him to hurt me anymore.

I fall at his feet and he kneels down on his haunches before running a hand over my hair. "Learn your place, little mouse, and I won't have to do this again."

He stands once more and I hear his fly unzip. "Now suck me. *Don't* get any blood on my cock."

I lift myself to my side before I grip his legs and inch my trembling body up to my knees. *Everything hurts*. I remember saying this to myself when I practiced for competition, but this pain is like no other.

This pain goes all the way to my soul. My will to survive is quickly becoming a fond memory.

How am I going to survive *this*? How is my heart, my body and my mind going to overcome *this*?

Once I'm on my bruised knees, I try to open my mouth wide several times for him, but I can't, and I soon realize that it's because my face is horribly swollen.

He scoffs and pushes me down onto my side. "See? Worthless."

I watch as he walks to the dresser and retrieves his pajamas. Shortly after that, he starts the shower as my limp body becomes one with the floor. Then, he gets into bed and turns off the light.

"Don't bother coming to bed," he snaps.

I close my eyes and allow a sweet memory to play behind my swollen eyelids.

"You are my sunshine, my only sunshine. You make me happy when skies are gray. You'll never know, dear, how much I love you. Please don't take my sunshine away."

I smiled as my tiny hands clutched my mother's robe. Her dark hair tickled my face and smelled like apples when she rocked me back and forth.

"Mama, why did you choose to be a doctor?"

She rested her cheek against the top of my head as she squeezed me gently. "Because I like helping people when they're hurt."

"Like you help me when I'm hurt?"

She giggled and kissed my hair before lifting me and placing me underneath my mermaid blanket. "Exactly."

She ran a soft hand over my cheek before kissing my forehead. "Happy birthday, my angel."

Dimitri left just as the sun began to rise, and I watched as the light spread across the floor, inching its way toward my battered body before the sunlight swallowed me whole. I allowed the rays of light to kiss my broken body and soothe my soul.

I laid like that for hours. When the maid came, she glanced at me before diverting her eyes and tidying up Dimitri's room. I thought that the people in this home had forgotten me, and I was thankful for it. But that wasn't the case. Someone did remember the girl who had been stolen.

Vadim.

"What has he done?" Vadim murmurs as he kneels down before me. His eyes travel over my body before they find mine. "Come, krasavaya. Let's get you cleaned up."

I wince as he tucks his arms beneath my back and legs before lifting me. He holds me to his chest as he carries me to the bathroom, and he sits me down gently at the vanity's bench before starting the bath.

Once the bath is full, he helps me to my feet before slowly lifting the dress over my head. His eyes grow wide at his first sight of my scathed body, but he quickly snaps out of it and removes my bra before helping me step out of my panties.

Vadim lifts me once more and I flinch once I'm lowered into the hot water. "I'm sorry, but it needs to be this hot to loosen up your muscles."

He stands and begins to leave, but I grasp his arm. I don't know why I do it. I don't want him to leave because, oddly enough, I feel safe in his presence. Even when I'm completely nude with bruises marking almost every inch of my body. In a way, I also want him to see the mistake that he made by taking me. I want him to feel remorse.

"Please stay," I croak.

He frowns as he slowly kneels once more beside the tub. "Sofia—"

I hold my hand up. "Just. Stay."

He nods as he stares down at the water, and I reach up and begin removing the pins from my hair, wincing every time I have to lift my arms higher.

"Let me," he murmurs, and then he begins carefully removing each pin, freeing several tendrils of hair at a time.

I reach for the vanilla scented body wash and hand it to him. "Will you?"

"Bathe you?" he breathes out.

I nod. "My arms are practically useless right now."

He shakes his head as his expression hardens. "This is inappropriate. You're to marry Dimitri."

"And what choice do I have in the matter?" I snap. "I *hate* him."

He scoffs. "You didn't look like you hated him when he fucked you at the end of the hall the other night."

I narrow my eyes at him. "Because my submission means that I don't get the shit beaten out of me."

Vadim sighs in defeat as he snatches the body wash from me. "I need a cloth."

I shake my head. "Use your hands."

"Absolutely not," he snaps.

"Why?" I retort. "Are you afraid to feel the marks that he left? All of this was your doing. You should have left me alone."

Vadim squeezes his eyes shut momentarily before squeezing the body wash into his hand. He hesitantly reaches towards me. It takes him a while to make contact with my skin, but when he does, I sigh. His gentle touch is what I need. It's a selfish desire, and I know that it's inappropriate on both ends, but it's more than wanting him to touch me where it hurts—I *need* him to undo what Dimitri did.

He begins at my neck before moving onto my shoulders. Then his hand trails to my chest, and he pauses with the weight of my breast in his palm. I gasp and lean into his touch as I close my eyes. He gently squeezes before running his thumb over the top of my breast.

"Vadim," I whisper, my eyes fluttering open to see his black eyes locked onto my face.

Gripping his wrist, I slide his hand over my stomach before submerging it into the water between my thighs. He sucks in a breath as he begins circling my clit slowly.

"More," I rasp, feeling that familiar need wind up in my womb.

He shoves his finger into my opening and I ride his hand like my life depends on it. But then, he pulls his finger out abruptly, leaving me breathless as he tangles his fingers in my hair and yanks my head back. The pain is unreal. My scalp feels like it's on fire and my neck is incredibly sore from Dimitri yanking me around like a ragdoll last night; the added pressure doesn't help in the least.

"What is your game, Sofia?" Vadim growls as his black eyes peer into mine.

I swallow hard, and I wonder if I'm about to take another beating. I'm not sure if I would survive it.

I shake my head slightly. "What do you mean?"

"You're trying to wiggle your way into my head, and I will not allow it," he sneers, shoving the body wash into my hand before he stands and leaves me alone.

My eyes burn and I realize that the need to cry is present, but I'm afraid I have no more tears to give.

Chapter 19

The Hunter will never be the Hunted

DIMITRI

I lock onto the beast as he saunters through the clearing of the woods surrounding my family's dacha. This East Siberian Brown Bear will be a prize. He's the largest that I've seen, and he'd be a beautiful addition to my collection.

When I left Sofia there, I didn't feel a thing. She should have been thankful, but she looked disgusted when I tried to offer her the ring. What was I to do? She had to be punished.

I couldn't face her this morning. I couldn't risk beating her again—at least not while my father is here. I already know that he isn't going to be pleased when he discovers what I've done, and the only reason is because of who she is. Once we're married, what I do to my wife will be nobody else's concern.

Initially, I wasn't happy about the arranged marriage, but after giving it some thought, I decided that it won't be so bad. As long as she continues to please me, and as long as she is grateful for my gifts … whatever they may be. I need to reel myself in, though. Where there is certainly a want to correct her—to harm her—I also do not wish to make her irreparable. She is the most beautiful woman I've ever seen. It's not just her looks, which are not comparable to any other pretty face I've locked eyes on, it's her drive. It's her desperate whims; when she thinks that she can manipulate *me* … when she thinks that she can destroy *me*.

I enjoy the challenge and I love the hunt. Sofia is no different than the large animal as I admire him from a distance. She is also the prize. I won't be stuffing her dead corpse and showcasing it in my office. No. The prize is her heart, her mind, and her soul. I want to possess her every thought and every word. That is true ownership, and it isn't just built on fear. Where fear is a necessity to garner respect, so is trust. I've got to condition her to trust me and fear me.

In order to stalk a bear, you must employ each and every hunting skill you've ever learned. You must move with the wind to avoid the bear's sharp nose, and you must be silent; playing on the sounds that the forest provides to trick the bear's keen ears. This is my place, and it's where I would come when I was a young boy every summer. It brings peace to my otherwise loud mind. It mends my madness. It silences the demons.

The bear stops and my finger tightens around the trigger as I hold my breath. He looks my way and doesn't bat an eye when I pull the trigger. The large, powerful beast falls to its side, as the blood trickles from his throat wound, and onto the permeable snow beneath his unmoving body.

Once I get back to the dacha, I suspend the bear in our gutting station, first removing his fur carefully and then his entrails, before cutting the meat from his bones.

As I'm about to prep him for stuffing, I hear snow crunching behind me as a result of hurried footsteps. When I turn, I'm welcomed by a fist to my jaw—igniting a fire to quickly spread throughout my body. I touch a finger to my lip before pulling it away and discovering my blood.

Vadim's chest hurriedly rises and falls in his exasperated state as he runs the back of his forearm across his mouth. "You are out of line, Dimitri!" he shouts. "You know who she is! You know what this marriage can do for our family—yet you beat her bloody?"

"She is *mine*!" I sneer as I approach him, still holding the hunting knife. My hands and forearms are soon to not only be covered in the bear's blood, but his as well.

"She is also the *daughter* of our biggest rival. It's imperative that she trusts us, Dimitri. The likelihood of her not running to her father is slim to none now that you've beaten the shit out of her. Did you not hear your father's wish, Dimitri? All of these years, her father has lied to her. He faked his death, and that alone would have given us leverage with Sofia and with him in turn. She won't forgive him, but she also won't think twice before running into his arms after what you've done!"

My chest heaves up and down as I ball my fists at my sides. "Where is my father?"

Vadim sighs as he leans against the table beside the suspended bear. "He had business to tend to in Moscow. He'll be back in several weeks to attend the wedding."

"And Sofia?"

He shakes his head slowly as he stares down at the bloodstained snow. "She's in your bed. She hasn't eaten all day. I ensured that she got cleaned up."

I nod before tossing the hunting knife onto the table that he's leaning on. I begin walking toward the house, but turn swiftly, wrapping my fingers tightly around his neck.

"Don't *ever* fucking touch me again or it will be the last thing you do, cousin. You're already treading on thin ice."

I enter the room quietly, and find her small form buried beneath the blanket. I remove my boots and walk to the bathroom before taking a quick shower.

She doesn't budge when I slip beside her beneath the blanket, but she flinches when I wrap my arm around her and pull her close before burying my nose into her hair. "YA izvinyayus' za skhozhu s uma." *I am sorry for losing my mind.*

She doesn't acknowledge my apology, and it angers me, causing my arm to tighten around her. She lets out a shaky breath, and I know that I'm hurting her.

"Sofia," I warn.

She nods slowly before whispering, "YA v poryadke." *I'm fine.*

"Turn around," I murmur, lifting my arm slightly to allow her to roll over.

She hesitates, but eventually follows my order. I look over her swollen face. Her brown eyes are surrounded with deep, purple bruises and her lip is busted. I did a number on her, and I'm thankful that my father isn't here to see what I've done.

I look into her glossy eyes and a smile pulls at my lips as I gently run my fingers over her bruised cheek. "I wouldn't have hurt you, Sofia. But *I* was hurt. You didn't want to accept my gift. My proposal went so differently in my head. When your face twisted in disgust … I lost my mind. I shouldn't have been so hard on you."

I inhale the scent of blood … of death, as Vlad flays the woman. Her screams are music, and I lift my arms and move them along to the classical music that plays along with her cries in the background.

I am the composer of death. The thought makes me smile.

It is nice to get my own hands bloody on occasion, but tonight I only wish to observe. The thought of flaying this woman was a result of me doing the same to the bear earlier. I have ideas that will not only fulfill my client's needs, but mine as well. This is only the beginning of *my* empire.

She hangs upside-down on an X shaped contraption that I built by hand. As per my orders, Vlad began cutting her from her sternum to her pelvic bone, and then after removing the skin from her abdomen, he continued to her arms and legs. The skin of her face, neck, hands and feet remain, but the rest of her body is pure muscle as it weaves into a sinewy design. Her body shakes from the shock and her eyes glitter with fear.

I nod to Vlad who retrieves the bucket of salt from the floor and begins dusting it over her body, causing her to twist awkwardly from side to side as she repeats the same sad song.

"Kill me! Please kill me!"

Eventually, they always beg for death.

Chapter 20

Fear Eats at Me

SOFIA

Two Weeks Later

“Today,” Vadim says as I look out at the falling snow. Each flake twirls gracefully before landing on the iced over lake outside.

He’s said the same thing every day since Dimitri assaulted me. He wants me to skate, but I’m afraid the will to find the release that the ice offers me simply isn’t there. I’m merely a shell of what I once was. My resolve is slowly dwindling. So many days and nights I’ve spent in this prison. I’m afraid that the second my blades touch the ice, I’ll be reminded of the life that had been stolen from me. I don’t want to give any of these men—not even Vadim—the chance to fill me with useless hope. The reality is, I’ll never compete again … I’ll never have freedom again.

When I slid Vadim's hand between my legs, I did so because I wanted a choice. I wanted, for once, to decide who touched me; who pleased me. I have never had that choice with Dimitri. Even in the hall that night, he would have taken me. He would have used me because that's what Dimitri does. He is only concerned about his own gain. He couldn't care less about me.

I feel Vadim's heat at my back as he approaches me, and I sigh when he rests a hand on my shoulder.

"Ne segodnya, Vadim." *Not today, Vadim.*

He gently places his index finger under my chin and tilts my head up. He stands tall as I sit in the chair with a fleece blanket wrapped around my shoulders.

"You will not survive this if you do not skate, Sofia."

His words make my heart flutter because they're true … but maybe I don't want to survive if there is no chance of escape.

"He won't let me go, Vadim. What's the point of skating if I can't have my freedom?"

A sad smile tugs at his lips as he points at the frigid lake outside. "That is your freedom, krasavaya. That is your destiny. It's where you belong."

My eyes once again travel to the lake as I contemplate his words. The ice is my destiny. It is where I belong, and though the thought is frightening, maybe he's right. If I can dig my soul from the depths of darkness where it hides, maybe I'll be more resilient to Dimitri's blows. Perhaps I'll break through the cocoon that he's wrapped me in and emerge as a magnificent butterfly, free from all restraints. The thought is bittersweet.

Life has become a dream … a goal. Because this isn't living.

"Okay," I murmur as I shake the blanket from my shoulders.

"Today?" he asks, and I nod my head, allowing a smile to curl my lips.

"Today."

Vadim meets me at the front door once I change into some fleece leggings and a sweater. I wear my hair down and lift it so that he can slip a warm jacket over my shoulders. He offers me some white earmuffs and I look at him quizzically.

"Do you have an MP3 player, or maybe an iPod and headphones? I like to listen to music while I skate."

He glances at me sheepishly as he reaches into his pocket. Staring down at his shoes, he hands me the device and earbuds. "You had this that night."

That night. Yes, the night that he took me.

I frown as I stare down at my MP3 player. This little thing was such a huge part of my life, and I'm taken aback when the realization that I'm holding a piece of the old me in my hands hits me. It makes me mourn for the girl that I am now, yet it also makes me smile to have a part of who I once was. It makes me hopeful that, one day, I will be her again.

"You've been keeping this in your pocket?" I ask, and his eyes travel to mine as he tucks his hands in his pockets.

"I have."

"Why?" I implore.

He sighs as he runs a hand over his shaved head. "Because, I—"

Dimitri startles me as he descends the stairs. "My beautiful little mouse is finally spreading her wings."

I force a smile as he wraps an arm around my waist and pulls me to his side. "I would stick around and watch, but I have business to attend to."

Vadim narrows his eyes at him. "What business?"

"Don't worry, cousin. It's business regarding the brothel. We're in need of some new girls. The others are washed up whores."

I bite the inside of my cheek as his words sink in. Brothel? Prostitutes? Not only do these men produce snuff films, but they are also involved in sex trade—illegal sex trade—and these girls are probably underage and here against their will. It makes me sick to my stomach.

Dimitri grabs my jaw and presses his lips to mine before turning and ascending the stairs. "I'll see you in my room tonight, Sofia. Be there at 7 PM sharp. Do not be late. I have a surprise for you."

I let out a slow breath as my eyes find Vadim's. "His surprises scare me."

Vadim nods slowly as he places a hand on my lower back and leads me out the front door. I stop and inhale the crisp winter's air. It's been weeks since I've been outside, and the sense of freedom is overwhelming as the flakes of snow drift from the sky and kiss my cheeks.

"He's an animal," I murmur as we stand on the porch surrounding the large home.

"He's also infatuated with you, krasavaya."

I smile at his words. "Always krasavaya …" I hold up my hands and quote him mockingly. "*Krasavaya, krasavaya, krasavaya.*"

"Do you blame me?" he asks as he leads me toward the frozen lake.

I tilt my head as I look up at him. "Blame you?"

"You are beautiful," he remarks, and I blush.

"You call me beautiful now, but I was nothing but cattle to you when you took me."

He stops us beneath a large, drooping tree. The snow that's gathered threatens to break the branches clean in half.

"I regret it, Sofia. The unfortunate truth is that I have taken many, but I also never had a chance to get to know them … like you."

I huff, sending my breath tumbling out like smoke from my lips as a result of the cold. "You never had to take me, Vadim. You chose to. You killed my uncle. You *ruined* my life."

"You're right," he remarks, placing a hand on my shoulder and leading me further from the estate. "But I can try to make up for it."

I step towards the frozen lake, and he hands me the skates that he bought me. "You'll never make up for it, Vadim. I'm here because of you."

"You've made it apparent," he says, and I whip around to face him.

"What do you expect?"

"Nothing," he breathes out. "I expect nothing, but I'd like it if you'd at least try."

I smirk as I sit on a tree stump and remove my shoes. "You're lucky that I don't deck you in the face right now. I have a history of doing so," I say, removing my shoes and lacing up my new skates.

"I'd deserve it if you did," he says as my gaze meets his.

"Oh? Why do you say that?"

"Because, you're a phoenix. And I'm afraid you'll shake off the ashes and destroy us all."

“Yeah?” I say, allowing my feet to glide across the ice. “You have no idea.”

VADIM

She is the equivalent of a rising angel. She will be my undoing.

DIMITRI

“Deeper,” I sigh as the new whore’s mouth moves up and down my shaft.

I grab at her golden hair and imagine that she is my future wife. “Yes,” I growl as she eagerly takes me deep into her throat. Then, she gags and my attention is lost.

“Get the fuck out!” I snap, and the girl’s frightened wide eyes find mine.

“I–I’m sorry, sir. I can try again. Did I do something wrong?” she pleads. Her whiny voice annoys me.

“Get. The. Fuck. Out,” I growl, narrowing my eyes at her.

She scurries off of the floor before grasping her clothing and holding it over her bare chest. Once she runs from the room frantically, I zip up my fly before standing and approaching the window.

My eyes drift from the snowcapped pine trees to the lake below. Leaning against the window, I sigh as I watch Sofia glide, spin, and jump.

SOFIA

When my new blades first touched the ice, I was hesitant to let myself be free. However, while I'm still imprisoned within the dacha's perimeter, I finally have my frozen stage beneath my feet. When *Crystalize* by Lindsey Stirling begins to play, I allow myself to feel the music once again.

Closing my eyes, I do an old set that I performed before at competition. I turn and glide backwards on the ice before kicking off and spinning, landing the Toe Loop.

Next, I go for a triple axel. One of the hardest jumps to perform, because you take it head on which adds a half rotation making it three and a half rotations—but I land it.

My soul roars as I allow myself to *feel* again … to *be.* I don't allow Dimitri or Vadim to cloud this moment. This moment belongs to me, and only me.

I don't think I've ever reached this kind of height with my jumps before and in the figure skating world, that is a good thing. A *very* good thing. If I were at a competition performing like this, I'd get bonus points for jumping 'beautifully'—beautiful meaning that I'm reaching major height and I'm covering *a lot* of ice. This lake is about the size of a football field, so I take full advantage. My speed is that of a freight train and my technique is on point, more than it's ever been.

The pieces of me have not been lost, and I cling to them with a vice grip. For the first time since being here, I'm convinced that I will not be broken. I will not be destroyed. Though it doesn't make me proud, I may have to play Dimitri's game of cat and mouse. In order to survive, I must do things that I'm not proud of.

I concentrate on running the razor upwards one last time before lowering my leg back into the steaming water. At "7 PM sharp," I went to Dimitri's room and discovered a white clothing box on the neatly made bed. A letter set atop the box and it read:

I'll be here at 8 pm, little mouse. Get cleaned up.

-Dimitri

I have no idea what his surprise could be and, frankly, I'm afraid to find out. It seems that Dimitri's intentions are never good.

Once I get out of the shower, I dry my hair and curl the ends, leaving it down before applying my makeup. Then, I open the box. Inside, I find a lacy, black brassiere and a matching thong. Below the lingerie, there is a very tight, and very short, red dress along with some crystal-embellished, suede Louboutin pumps that probably cost him an arm and a leg.

I dress myself and then stare up at the antique grandfather clock on the far side of the room. My heart picks up the pace as I await his arrival. *Two minutes.*

The door cracks open, and I stare up at him. He's wearing a tuxedo and it's tailored to perfection. I can nearly make out his muscles as he stands before me. His usually amuck hair is combed suavely to the side in classic fashion. He takes my breath away and, for a moment, I almost forget the monster that he is.

"You look absolutely stunning," he breathes out as he slowly approaches me. "You are going to be the most beautiful bride in Russian history."

Placing his index finger under my chin, he lifts my face to his. He has astonishing eyes, they're like burning embers. They hold no truth, or promise. They have an uncertainty about them.

I lick my lips. "You look very handsome."

He smiles as his eyes drift to my lips. "It's time to go, little mouse."

I nod as he grabs my hand and leads me through the hall and down the stairs. I'm shocked when we turn the corner and enter a room that I've never been in before.

A table for two awaits us. It's covered in black silk, matching the rest of the gothic style room. Sconces line the walls, and the very dim lighting is accompanied by soft candlelight.

Dimitri places a hand on my lower back and leads me further into the room. "I wanted to make-up for that night, little mouse," he says, pulling out a chair and allowing me to sit.

I divert my eyes as he slides onto the chair across from me. "This is nice. Thank you."

Thanking this man for anything makes my insides coil, but I'm playing his game of hot, cold, hot, cold. I've got to keep my head straight, because his certainly is not.

One of the maids walks into the room and pours us each a glass of red wine. The pungent smell hits my nostrils. I'm not a drinker. I've tried before when mom would occasionally offer me a sip, but I've never been a fan of the tart taste of potent wine.

"Tonight, we're having Shashlik. It's skewered meat. Have you ever had it?"

I shake my head slowly as I lift the wine glass and press it to my lips, hoping that the wine will wet my pallet, but it only makes it drier.

"How are you liking Russia?" he asks, and I almost scoff at him, but I reel it in.

How do I *like* Russia? Is he serious?

I force a smile. "I love it. I'm learning a lot."

"I saw you skating earlier. You are very talented. You reminded me of a bird in flight. You definitely make the art look simple, which says a lot about your skill. Vadim said you've competed?"

I nod. "I've been competing since I was a little girl. I started off being a sweeper, collecting roses and stuffed animals for each program."

"What made you want to figure skate?" he asks, and I frown.

He wants to know about me for once?

"It's where I'm supposed to be."

He surveys me with his eyes for several seconds and I fidget awkwardly in my chair.

"Do I make you uncomfortable, Sofia?"

My eyes dart up to his. "No … well, sometimes I guess."

"Am I making you uncomfortable now?"

My eyebrows pinch together as I contemplate his question. "Yes," I whisper.

"Why?" he asks, his tone unreadable.

I sigh. "Because I'm not used to you being like this."

His hand creeps across the table before he grasps mine and circles his thumb around the diamond that I wear. "You're going to be my wife, and I do not wish for you to fear me. I want your devotion. I want your admiration and your love."

After dinner, Dimitri leads me back to his room. I sigh when he steps behind me and trails kisses from my neck to my shoulder.

"I want you in every way," he rasps. His breath sweeps across my flesh, leaving tingles behind.

He helps me step out of the pumps before unzipping the dress down the back. Dimitri slowly pulls it down, kissing every inch of skin that becomes exposed before turning me around to face him.

"Sofia," he whispers, his lips hovering above mine. "Tell me that you want me, that you want this."

I gasp when he squeezes my breasts in his large hands. "I–I want you. I want this."

He runs a hand up my neck to the back of my hair before tangling his fingers in the strands. "You better not be lying to me, little mouse."

I shake my head slowly. "I want you, Dimitri. I want this." Reaching up, I trail an index finger over his strong jaw to his thick lips. "When will you believe me, *my love*?"

His cognac eyes watch me carefully as I bite my lip seductively. "I shouldn't have acted the way that I did that night, when we had dinner with your family. Your gift was beautiful, and I should have acted accordingly."

My hand falls to his bow tie and I untie it before slowly unbuttoning his crisp white shirt. "You're the most handsome man that I've ever seen." I lean down and kiss his chest before running my tongue to his sternum. "I want you inside of me."

He growls as he rips his dress shirt and jacket from his shoulders. His lips slam into mine and I frantically grab at his belt as he backs me towards the bed.

Dimitri lifts me and tosses me onto the bed before he covers my body with his. He reaches behind me and unclasps my bra before ripping it from my body. His eyes never leave mine as he leans down and takes my nipple into his mouth. I sigh and arch my back as he circles his tongue around my areola, then he moves on to the other before trailing a kisses down my stomach.

He slightly pulls my panties down on one side before sucking, nipping, and kissing the sensitive skin. I moan as he teases me, and he finally sits up and places a thumb under the sides of my panties before pulling them down my legs.

He grips the backs of my thighs before pushing my knees to the bed. “This is mine,” he murmurs as he observes my pussy. “Understand, that if anyone ever touches what is mine, I will fucking kill them in the most horrific way—and you will watch every second.”

My breath hitches when his head dips down between my thighs and he takes my clit into his mouth. The foreplay left me sated, so it doesn’t take long for an orgasm to sweep through me like a tsunami.

“Please,” I breathe out.

Dimitri crawls over me and I feel the head of his cock at my entrance. “Please what?”

“Please fuck me,” I say, staring him in the eye.

A smug smile crosses his face as he slowly stretches me. I reach behind him and grip his back, digging my nails into his flesh. He begins fucking me furiously as I slide my nails down his muscles to the small of his back. I place my palm flat against his lower back as he pounds into me. I tighten around his length, causing a moan to roll from his lips.

He flips over, taking me with him. “Ride me, little mouse.”

I begin rolling my hips, causing his massive length to go deeper than it ever has. “Oh my God,” I rasp as I pick up the pace.

I stare up at the ceiling, trying to imagine that I’m fucking somebody else passionately, but the reality is—I don’t want to. Trying to convince myself that I do not enjoy Dimitri’s fuck sessions would be a lost cause, because I do. I thoroughly enjoy being ravaged by this man. A monster he is, but his masculine beauty is undeniable. I tried to fool him tonight, yet I only fooled myself into believing that my trickery would work.

My gaze falls to his as his fingers dig into my hips. I allow my eyes to trace his handsome face. From his strong brow to his hooded eyes to his solid jaw and thick lips—he is perfection. How a demon can be wrapped in such beauty is beyond me.

He sits up and grasps my lower back before pulling my lips to his. He kisses me feverishly as he leads my movements, and my need soars before ecstasy crashes down around me. I pull my lips from his as I erupt around his length, crying out my captor’s name.

Chapter 21

Whispering Secrets

"No!" I breathe out when I enter the library.

Vadim gently grasps my arm when I try to back out. "It's not what you think it is, Sofia. You're going to sit in the chair and state your name, your parents' names, and confirm that you are to marry Dimitri Vavilov. That's it."

"Why?" I implore as I look up at him.

His jaw tenses as he becomes frustrated with me. "Because. Now go sit and do as I say."

I frown as he leads me to the chair. I sit and lean back as he steps behind the video camera mounted on a tripod.

"Smile," he says as he eyes me.

I give him the fakest smile I can muster and he narrows his eyes at me. My shoulders slump as I huff, then, as ordered, I straighten my back and give him a relaxed smile. He nods as he begins recording.

I swallow hard as I play up my act. “My name is Sofia Dmitriev. I am the daughter of the late David and Lidiya Dmitriev. I am to marry Dimitri Vavilov.”

He smiles as he stops the recording. “See? That wasn’t that hard.”

“I don’t understand why I had to do that, Vadim. Why did I have to state my parents' names? What is going on?”

He walks towards me before reaching down for my hand. “You ask too many questions.”

“Yeah, because it isn’t human nature to ask questions,” I quip, and he chuckles as he helps me up.

“How are you and Dimitri getting along?”

I sigh as my hand slips from his and I approach the window. “We’re getting along great. He’s a happy camper as long as I fuck him … *willingly*.”

Vadim steps beside me, his shoulder touches mine and it sends shivers down my spine. “Why did you stop me that day, Vadim? When I was in the bath?”

He sighs. "You know why I stopped you, Sofia. Don't be ignorant."

"Ignorance is bliss," I murmur, my eyes remaining fixed on the lake outside.

I feel his breath against my cheek as he looks towards me. "I think the better question is why you wanted me to touch you in the first place."

"Comfort," I respond immediately. "A choice."

"That's it?"

I look up into his eyes. "I'm sure I could give you a list of other reasons, but then I'd be ignorant," I say, lifting my hands and quoting him mockingly as my gaze travels back to the window.

"I'm much older than you," he whispers.

I nod. "I know that."

"I'm also a married man, and you're soon to be a married woman."

"You're married?" I ask, tilting my head to the side as I look at his reflection in the window.

He nods. "Eleven years."

"Where is she now?"

He shrugs. “It doesn’t matter. Not anymore.”

I frown as I turn to face him. “Is she alive?”

“Barely.”

“I’m not following.”

He smiles weakly as his eyes sober. “You don’t need to. Now come. There is a very busy day ahead.”

“There are four steps to a Russian wedding,” Alina says as she curls my hair. “First, the groom must pay the ransom. We call it vykup nevesty. Then, there is the traditional ceremony, known as venchanie, which is held in a church. But yours will be held in our family’s chapel. It’s divided in two parts; the betrothal and the crowning. After that, there’s the civil ceremony called rospis v zagse. That usually takes place at the department of public services, but we know a man who will come here. It’s tradition to tour the city after the civil ceremony, and I imagine Dimitri will allow that. Basically, you are escorted around the city in a limo to look at the sights. Then, my favorite part,” she says excitedly as she runs her fingers through my hair.

I frown at her. “What?”

"The reception!" she squeaks. "Our family's tradition is a grand ball. We all wear masks."

"Like a masquerade?"

She nods. "Exactly. And I'm happy to say that I will be your stylist throughout the entire event. Now," she says as she exits the bathroom momentarily before returning with a white, flowing gown. "This is what you will wear for when Dimitri pays the ransom. Usually, he would be going to your family home to do so, but …" She eyes me solemnly in the mirror. "We will be doing that here."

I change into the dress before she rests the crown made of entwined flowers atop my head. The empire waist dress is simple, yet beautiful as it sweeps the ground.

"You look stunning, Sofia," Alina whispers as she steps behind me.

I stand at the top of the stairs as I watch the commotion below. When Dimitri enters the home, he has a small jewelry box with him as he pretends to look for me. The Pakhan nods to an open door, and a large man enters wearing a veil. When Dimitri lifts the veil, he mocks exasperation as he begins running to the other members of the family. He shakes their shoulders and repeats, "Where is my love?"

Alina takes my hand and begins leading me down the stairs. Dimitri stops his antics and stares up at me as I descend down each step. A smile curls his lips when Alina stops me in front of him.

"There she is," he whispers as he places the jewelry box in my hands. I open the box and sigh when I see the charm bracelet inside. Each charm represents a piece of me … an ice skate and a music note, but when I see the lock without a key, I frown.

Dimitri grabs my hand and leads me down a hall that I've never been down before. I look behind me and see the family still waiting in the foyer, watching us eagerly.

He stops at a door at the very end before looking down at me. "I hope that you like the ransom that I paid for your hand, little mouse."

He steps forward and pushes the door open, and I almost fall to my knees at what I find.

"It's your very own frigid sanctuary, Sofia."

My eyes travel around the indoor ice rink. It's about the size of a basketball court, and absolutely incredible. The ice looks purple, and a spotlight shines down right in the center. Windows surround the room, and speakers are mounted in every corner.

"How did you do this?" I breathe out.

"Money, Sofia. Money and power. I can give you the world if you allow it."

My eyes travel to his. "It's perfect. Thank you."

Dimitri smiles before leaning down to kiss me softly.

"You're welcome."

The family's chapel is absolutely stunning. It's another place that I have yet to discover in this massive home until now.

The dome ceiling is painted with angels and clouds, and as we stand at the entrance of the church, I admire the floor to ceiling paintings of saints and biblical stories.

I stand to the left of Dimitri as we each hold a lit candle for the betrothal. The deacon leads the litany before saying two prayers. After that, the rings that were blessed prior to the ceremony are placed on each of our right ring fingers.

The priest says another prayer, blessing our betrothal.

Holy Matrimony is considered a Sacred Mystery in the Eastern Orthodox Church, and the sign of marriage isn't the exchange of rings like it is in the states. It's having a crown placed on the bride and groom's head.

The deacon leads us to the nave, where we stand on a rose colored rug. Dimitri professes that he is marrying me of his own free will and that there is no other. I am forced to do the same as I choke back resentful tears.

After several more prayers, the crowns are placed on top of our heads before the priest shares a chalice of wine with Dimitri and me.

My fate is almost sealed.

Almost.

The civil ceremony is held in one of the sitting rooms where we are greeted by Dimitri's family. They are holding bread and salt, which I'm assuming is a Russian tradition.

This time, Dimitri slips the ring on my finger before I do the same to his. We're each given a crystal glass, and Dimitri demonstrates as he throws it onto the ground, shattering it. I do the same, jumping back as the shards of glass shatter against the hard floor.

Dimitri grabs my waist before whispering into my ear, "Do you see how many shards there are? We are to have a very happy marriage, Sofia."

We step outside with Dimitri's family in tow, and we are each given a white dove. When we set them free, I envy the birds as they spread their wings and fly towards the heavens. Then, I'm given a white balloon. I soon realize that my surname is written on the balloon in cursive, and I know what I'm to do.

I allow a single tear to escape my eye as I watch the balloon float up and away towards the grey sky.

I'm no longer Sofia Dmitriev. I am Sofia *Vavilov*.

Chapter 22

Traditions

I stare down at the sea of people. They're all wearing masks, and the women wear elegant gowns that look as if they're from the eighteenth century. The men do as well in their breeches and coats … some wear cravats and some wear cloaks.

The point of a masquerade is to hide—to be discreet—and it's the most comfortable that I've felt since I've been here. I prefer to stay hidden behind the cream colored lace mask that covers the upper part of my face.

Dimitri isn't hard to spot, though. He wears a black cloak with a three sided hat tilted at the side. His mask is magnificent; it only covers half of his face and is lined with silver, the majority of it being black. His strong energy emanates from him. The mask doesn't hide what he is—incredibly handsome and *evil*. The women don't seem to mind the monster that he is, or they just don't care because they flock to him like bees to honey.

Alina made sure that we didn't see each other after he 'allowed' me to tour the city with him. Ironically, this home is very close to Moscow; the same place that I originally landed when I first came to Russia. We never left the limo, but he showed me St. Basil's Cathedral and Moscow Kremlin. All I could do was look on silently as he went on about their unique architecture.

The Rococo styled ballroom is breathtaking. The few pieces of ornate furniture are situated in the corners for the guests to sit and mingle. The architecture is lighter and more graceful than the rest of the home. The walls are white with leafy, stucco designs, and the floor is a dark, cherry wood.

A braided staircase wraps around beautifully and it leads to a balcony. That's where I'm currently hiding, hoping that I'm not spotted.

The gown that I wear is stunning. The silver fabric reminds me of fish scales, and my breasts nearly threaten to spill from the corset. The long, soft, black feathers that are pinned in my hair curl slightly and occasionally tickle my cheeks.

"You can only hide for so long, krasavaya."

I turn and see Vadim standing inches away from me. He is wearing a burgundy cloak and a classic, black masquerade mask. The nose is long, and it only covers the upper half of his face.

"I've been spotted," I murmur, before turning and grasping the rail once more.

He steps beside me and sighs. "You should go entertain your husband. He'll be upset if he has to come find you."

I scoff as I look towards Dimitri. He's one man in a sea of women. "He looks pretty entertained already."

Vadim chuckles. "You're jealous?"

I frown as I stare at my *husband*. "No. I just think it's unfair. I wonder how many other women he's had since I've been here. The fact that I don't have that same right is frustrating to say the least."

"As if there are any other men you have your eyes set on. Dimitri is a bastard, but he's never had a hard time getting any woman he wants."

Just as I'm about to spout off, I see a familiar face, and my heart feels as if it's lodged in my throat.

"Boris," I murmur as I turn and begin making my way down the stairs.

"Boris?" Vadim says as he follows behind me.

I bunch the gown in my hands as I begin hurrying down the steps. I'm feet away from him when an arm wraps around my waist. I look up into Dimitri's eyes as he swiftly turns me to face him.

"Where are you running off to?"

My eyes frantically search around, but I can no longer see Boris, the boy from the village. The one who always ran away.

I look into Dimitri's eyes and smile. "I was looking for you."

He smiles as his eyes drift to my crimson lips. "Tonight, we are going to go spend some time at my cabin in the woods. I'll take you there by horseback."

"Oh?" I whisper as he places a finger beneath my chin.

"I have another gift for you," he murmurs, before leaning down and kissing my jaw.

"Now," he says, taking my hand in his. "Let's paint on our smiles and get this over with."

The crowd begins clearing and lining the walls. My eyes search the masked faces for the simple, white half-mask that Boris was wearing. I see nothing but women who are obviously sneering at me. I guess they prefer to be with my monster of a husband, and I'd happily give him to them.

The Pakhan waits in the center of the room where a table is wheeled out to him. We stand, facing him, on the other side of the table as he begins filling three shot glasses. He retrieves one glass, and Dimitri picks up the other two, handing me one.

"To my only son and the newest addition of our family, Sofia Vavilov. May you have a happy, full marriage."

The crowd begins chanting, "*Gorko, gorko, gorko*," which is Russian for bitter, and Dimitri and his father slam back their drinks. I'm lost in the confusion, but quickly wrap my head around what I'm supposed to do. The vodka burns my throat, causing me to grimace. I gasp when Dimitri's lips slam into mine and his tongue darts into my mouth. It feels like my lips are becoming bruised as he holds me against him. When he pulls away, it takes me a moment to catch my breath.

"It will help with the taste," he whispers, before winking and releasing me.

This time, Dimitri fills the shot glasses before he hands me mine once more. I'm dreading another shot. I already feel nauseous from the last one.

I hold my glass up as Dimitri toasts, "To my father, the Pakhan."

His father nods, and this time I down my shot along with the two men.

The table is wheeled away and the Pakhan leaves with it, leaving Dimitri and I alone in the middle of the ballroom.

He grasps my lower back and pulls me close to him as a slow waltz begins to play. He leads my movements, and it isn't long for me to catch on. In order to be a figure skater, you must also be a dancer.

Dimitri looks mysterious and handsome as he spins me several times before pulling me into his arms. "You look incredible, my love. I had expectations for what my wife would be. They were very high, but you've surpassed them."

I frown as I look up into his eyes. Just as I'm about to respond, the crowd closes in on us and begins slowly chanting "*kalinka, kalinka, kalinka*" as a different song begins to play.

Dimitri backs away and bows to me. It makes me smile as he holds his arms out in front of him before placing one forearm over the other. He nods for me to do the same and I do, then he begins tapping one heel on the floor before doing the same to the other. I follow his movements, and the pace quickens as the song speeds up. The crowd is no longer slowly chanting "*kalinka,*" but hollering it as they clap their hands to our movements.

I laugh as Dimitri links an arm through mine and begins running around in a circle, taking me with him. I'm dizzy when he grabs my waist and begins twirling me. The alcohol kicks in as a result of my movements, causing me to feel loose and happy. It feels *good.*

Once the song ends, the crowd goes wild as Dimitri pulls me into his arms. A charming smile spreads over his face, and I don't know if it's from the alcohol or the celebratory feel in the air, but it makes me melt inside.

Dimitri grasps my arm as I trip over a stray branch. I stop and laugh, grabbing my stomach as I lean against a large tree.

"You seemed to have had fun, little mouse," he murmurs.

I look towards him through droopy eyelids. I'm drunk. *Drunk.* I've never felt this way before, and it's somewhat freeing. Especially after everything. I let one more laugh bubble from my gut before pushing from the tree and grabbing his extended hand.

"That was a lot of fun."

He chuckles. "It's too bad you stayed hidden in the balcony for the majority of the celebration. I was waiting for you to come down and claim me as your husband."

I nearly trip again and he catches me around my waist. I look into his eyes and frown. "You're the most confusing man that I've ever met."

"Confusing? I think that I've been straight forward, mouse."

"You're not very nice," I say under my breath as we approach a stable, but I'm sure he heard me because he cocks his eyebrow.

My breath catches in my throat when I see a beautiful horse pawing the ground as its being saddled. Its pure white without any trace of color. Its mane is long and hangs over its neck while its tail sweeps the dusty snow which has covered the ground.

"Do you like her?" Dimitri whispers.

I can't take my eyes away. She's absolutely stunning; she almost doesn't seem real. "She–she's beautiful."

"She's yours," he responds nonchalantly as he leads me to her.

Her dark eyes lock onto mine as she stills her foot. Dimitri places a hand on my lower back before pushing me towards her. Her nostrils flare as she exhales, and it looks like smoke billows from them as a result from the cold.

I reach out and she eyes my hand as it lingers over her long nose. She hesitates before bumping my palm, and I run a hand from her nose to her jaw. "Pegasus," I whisper. "Her name is Pegasus."

Dimitri laughs. "Pegasus was a stallion. Not a mare."

"She'll take me to heaven," I whisper, ignoring his statement.

He steps around me before mounting Pegasus. He reaches down, and I grasp his forearm as he lifts me onto her back behind him.

"Hold on," he says, looking behind him momentarily.

I wrap my arms around his waist as he nudges Pegasus' side with his heel. Once we merge into the darkness of the forest, I watch the traces that the trees leave behind. I try to catch them as they pass me, but as Pegasus' muscles work quickly beneath me, each tree is fast going as my new friend leads me to my fate. I don't know which Dimitri I'll face tonight. I never do.

Once we get to a small, wooden structure, Dimitri slides off of the horse before grasping my waist. My chest brushes against his as he lowers me to my feet. He's still wearing the cloak and his messy hair makes him look boyish. Looks alone, he reminds me of a prince. The thought is silly. If he's a prince, then he's The Prince of Darkness. And I'm the sacrifice; the lamb that will be bled dry to feed his power.

He leads Pegasus to a small stable behind the cabin before removing the saddle and brushing her back. Once she's all set in the stall, he grasps my hand and leads me into the cabin as he holds a lantern in front of him.

When I follow him inside, my eyes travel around the warm surroundings. The windows have sheer curtains hanging over them, and the floor is weathered. The large bed takes up most of the space and is covered in a brown fur.

Dimitri sets the lantern down before walking towards a wood burning stove in the corner of the room. Once the fire comes to life, the small room begins to warm, allowing me to slip the heavy cloak from my shoulders before removing the long, black gloves.

His back faces me as he turns his head slightly. "Take your hair down, Sofia."

I let out a shaky breath as I begin pulling the pins from my hair as he pours us each a drink. Just as he turns, I remove the last pin and place it on the small, round table along with the others.

His face holds a serious expression as he approaches me with the drinks. "You did incredible today," he murmurs as he hands me my drink.

I take it from him hastily, eager to lose myself in the haze that the alcohol offers me. I've always been afraid to drink. To lose my inhibitions and potentially get into trouble … to make life altering decisions that cannot be reversed. None of that matters anymore. The girl who was once so careful is hiding away, watching me with sober eyes, but I don't care. *She* was careful, yet, she still ended up having the unthinkable happen to her.

I slam back the drink before slamming the glass onto the surface of the table. Wiping the back of my forearm over my mouth, I look into Dimitri's gaze as he regards me.

He smirks before he allows the contents of the glass to slide down his throat then turns and retrieves the vodka. This time, he fills my glass with double the amount, but he only fills his halfway before nodding to my glass. I turn my nose up as I snatch the glass from the table, causing the vodka to slosh over the sides before taking it all in with several gulps.

I gasp and stumble backwards when the burn hits my stomach. In a flash, Dimitri grasps my shoulders in his large hands. His face hovers over mine, and I tilt my head back, brushing my lips against his.

Reaching up, I place my hands on each side of his face before my eyes travel up to his. His jaw tenses and his eyelids are heavy as his cognac irises peer out from beneath his long, black eyelashes.

"How can you make me feel this way?" I whisper into the inch between our lips.

Dimitri smiles and brushes his nose against mine. "I would ask you the same thing, little mouse," he rasps as his fingers drift from my collarbone to my cleavage. "But, sometimes, you have to let the inevitable happen."

My breath hitches when he rips my dress down the center. His lips find mine, and I tangle my fingers in his hair as I allow him to diminish every ounce of hesitation on my part. The ripped dress slides over my hips as he backs me to the bed, his lips not once leaving mine. When he lays me down, he pulls his mouth from mine as he stands straight and removes his cloak followed by his shirt. He's only wearing his breeches and boots as he stares down at me with a hunger that I've not seen before in his eyes.

I'm quickly learning that my resolve is a fickle thing. I was forced to come to this place and made to marry, along with all of the in-betweens. Yet, through it all, I still open my legs for this man. I'm headstrong, yet temperamental. I'm yo-yoing between what's right, and what's wrong. It's a never-ending cycle, and it's all Dimitri's doing.

I've yet to discover if he has a heart. If he does, it's cold and black at best.

What made him turn into a bloodthirsty, volatile monster is beyond me—and I'm not even sure if he *was* ever different. Maybe monsters like him are born with a relentless thorn in their side; a nagging that never lets down … a hunger that can never be satisfied.

When I look up into his eyes, I want to find out. I want to open him up and see what makes him tick. He's psychotic, yet magnificent. He's a conundrum, and I will make it my mission to solve him … to uncover his truth. Though I'm sure it's riddled with cobwebs and lies and deceit.

As he stands before me, I allow my eyes to trace every inch of his milky skin. From his hooded eyes, to his narrow nose, to his lush lips. His broad shoulders show me his strength, and his muscular arms evoke memories that I should be ashamed of. Those arms have trapped me, yet they have held me close as he's claimed me in so many ways.

From there, my eyes drift to his hard chest just before they linger over his abs where a thin trail of dark hair leads to the place that I've forbidden myself to think about, though I can't say the same for my dreams. He's always haunting them, and when I wake, my core is throbbing and the moisture between my thighs is a stark reminder of my sick attraction to him.

I sit up on my elbows, causing my breasts to push upwards from the restraining white corset that I wear. Reaching in front of me, I grab the silk ribbon that holds the corset together before pulling each strand from the bodice. His eager eyes watch each, slow movement as my lungs become unrestrained.

Dimitri begins removing his belt as he watches me, and I find myself watching him with the same voraciousness. We each want to consume each other. The evident desire is thick as it travels between our two bodies.

When I open the corset, a strangled growl escapes him as he holds his massive length in his hand. He strokes himself as I lie on my back once more before hooking my thumbs through my panties and pulling them over my legs.

I spread my legs wide and he watches as I reach between my thighs and run my middle finger between my wet folds. His head tilts to the side as I begin slowly circling my clit, my eyes staying locked on his face so I can see the desire written into his features.

Dimitri's grasp tightens around his cock as he stops himself and crawls onto the bed. He grasps my wrist before pulling my hand to his mouth. My fingers are still wet from my desire as he runs them across his bottom lip, his tongue darting out to taste me.

I sigh as I watch him run his tongue along each of my fingers like they're a delicacy. His body falls over me and I lean forward to capture his lips, but he pulls away, staring into my eyes intently as the head of his cock nudges my opening.

I moan as his width stretches me … slowly … tauntingly. I scratch at his back, eager for him to fill me, but he only smiles, stopping as he's only about halfway inside of my aching pussy.

His hands slide over my curves as he sits up on his knees. Grabbing my hips, he lifts my lower body and slams into me. I gasp and my back arches as his fingers squeeze my hips harshly. I look up into his eyes, and they shimmer with a primal need as he claims me. I grip the fur below me in my fists as I tighten around his length.

I remain tangled in the blankets as Dimitri stands. My eyes travel over his muscular back as he kneels down and grabs his pants from the floor.

He reaches into the pocket and retrieves a tiny bag before dropping the pants and walking back towards the bed. He opens the bag and leans over, dumping little piles of white dust onto the nightstand. He uses a card to form each bump into a thin line before rolling up a rectangular piece of paper.

He presses the rolled-up piece up paper to one nostril and pinches his other nostril shut with his index finger. The snorting sound fills the room as he sucks one line up his nose. He sits up and leans his head back as he stares at the ceiling.

"Come here," he mutters, reaching for me.

I sit up, holding the blanket to my chest as I scooch towards him. Dimitri wraps his arm around my waist before running his nose along the crook of my neck.

"I want you to try, mouse," he whispers against my flesh, holding the piece of rolled up paper in front of us.

I stare down at it. My conscience is obviously screaming at me as sober Sofia watches from afar with fearful eyes, not saying a word. My dead mother's face flashes in my mind as I reach for the paper.

Holding it in my hand, my eyes travel to the three remaining lines of cocaine.

"Just one," he whispers as he grabs my hips and nudges me closer to the table. "Don't think. Just suck it up your nose."

I purse my lips as I lean over the table, and Dimitri positions himself behind me as he pulls my hair over my shoulder.

"Go on," he says, his hard chest pressing against my back.

I hold the paper up to my nose and do exactly as Dimitri did earlier when he snorted the line. The cocaine is bitter, but surprisingly, it doesn't burn my nose as badly as I'd thought it would. The sensation is unlike any other as the numbness coats the back of my throat. I can't feel my teeth as I lean my head back on his shoulder and allow the paper to fall from my hand. Pure, unadulterated euphoria courses through my veins, and I smile.

"How do you feel?" Dimitri whispers against my cheek.

I turn my head slightly and stare into his eyes, wondering if mine look black like his.

"Amazing," I murmur, placing my hand over his cheek. "I want to do another one."

Chapter 23

Uncovering Truths

DIMITRI

"How are we looking?" my father mutters as he looks over the screen of his laptop.

I smile. "Much better than we were. The videos are in high demand. The need has grown immensely since we changed direction." I smirk at Vadim and he glares at me.

"This is very good news, Dimitri. I'm glad you're finally becoming invested in our family's business," the Pakhan says as he eyes me from over his laptop. "How are you and Sofia getting along?"

I sit back in the armchair and smile as my eyes travel to the window. "We are getting along just fine, papa. I must say, she is quite an amazing girl. We share more interests than I'd originally thought."

Vadim scoffs and my eyes snap to his. "If you have something to say, Cousin, then by all means—say it."

His jaw tenses as he runs his hand down his face.

That's what I thought.

"And Vadim, how is Boris getting along?"

Vadim looks toward him and sighs before slumping down in his chair. "He's doing fine. Better than I thought he would."

My father nods slowly as his desk phone begins to ring. He presses the speaker button. "Yes?"

"We have a visitor. David Dmitriev has come with his entourage. They're here to speak to you."

My father smiles deviously as his eyes travel between Vadim and I. "Pat them down and send them to my office."

It's been years since I've seen David Dmitriev and, unlike before, I catch myself observing his features—searching for any resemblance to Sofia.

She has his golden hair and brown eyes. She got the rest of her looks from Lidiya. He's accompanied by his son, Sofia's half-brother, and three of his men.

"Where is she?" David seethes, clenching his fists at his sides as his men stand behind him.

My father smirks at him. "All in due time," he says, before leaning forward. "We've had our differences in the past, David, but I'm hoping that we can mend the bridges. We are family now, after all."

David sighs in defeat. "She is married already then?"

My father nods pointedly to me. "Dimitri is to be the next Pakhan, and she is his wife. I can assure you that she has been well taken care of."

David glares at me. "Have you been good to my daughter?"

"Absolutely," I say sardonically. "And she has been good to me. Very, *very* good."

"You motherfucker," he growls, taking a step towards me.

"I wouldn't do that, David," Vadim says, calmly. "We are here to discuss our alliance with each other. Sofia is a beautiful, talented girl. I wouldn't want her to get caught up in unnecessary feuds between our families. As you know, they never go well."

A strangled growl escapes David as he hangs his shoulders slightly. "I want to see her."

"You will see her soon enough. First, we need to talk business," my father says, leaning back in his chair and steepling his fingers. "We would like a twenty-five percent cut of your bratva's earnings from here on out. We would also like for you to stay away from our clientele."

"Twenty-five percent?" Sofia's brother, Alexei, spits out. "You're insane."

David holds his hand up. "Done."

Alexei's wide eyes snap to his father and David gives him a stern look. "I will do whatever it takes to ensure that my daughter is safe." He looks towards my father. "Now, I would like to see Sofia."

Chapter 24

Bittersweet Symphony

SOFIA

I run my fingers along the spines of books as I walk the bookshelves of the library, waiting for Vadim to show. He's later than usual.

When I hear the door open, I smile. "Nice of you to finally show. I thought I was being stood-up."

When he doesn't respond, I turn, and the breath feels as though it's been sucked from my lungs.

It can't be. No. This is a dream. It must be .... It's either that, or this man eerily resembles a dead man.

The dead man being my father.

I place a hand flat on my abdomen as I stumble backwards, blindly reaching behind me to locate something to steady myself. *Breathe*. I can't. I can't will my lungs to function. All I see are memories dancing at the forefront of my vision. Memories that

I've pushed so far back, that I swore to never recall again.

The mind is a funny thing, locking away visions to keep them from haunting you, only to unleash them once you're triggered. I'd like to keep them buried forever.

"Sofia," he murmurs, taking a step towards me.

I hold a hand up as the tears flood my vision. "Who-who are you?"

My gaze drifts over his shoulder and I see another man. He must be several years older than me, but something about him makes me sense recognition … a bond of sorts as he looks at me solemnly.

"It's me," the older man whispers as he begins approaching me. "It's me, Sofia."

I hurriedly step around the armchair that Vadim usually occupies in an attempt to put something between us. "I don't know you."

"You do. I'm your father."

I shake my head emphatically. "No, you're not." I breathe out. "Don't say that!"

Hurt morphs his features. “Listen to me, Sofia. I am your father, and this is your brother Alexei.”

I laugh like a mad woman as I continue to shake my head, tears streaming down my cheeks. “No.”

“It’s true. Sofia, I’ve missed you so much. If you only knew. I didn’t have a choice.”

“No!” I scream, glaring at him. “My father is dead. He–he died when I was four. He had a brain aneurism … he … he ….”

“No,” he whispers, shaking his head slowly as a pained look spreads across his familiar features. “I didn’t. That isn’t the truth.”

My jaw tenses as I look at him. There isn’t any denying who he is. He is my father.

“You lied?” I choke out, staring up into his brown eyes, hoping and praying that this encounter isn’t real, because if it is, it means that my entire life has been a lie. Who allows their child to believe that they’re dead? So many nights, I would cry into my pillow, and I would talk to my dead father’s soul. I was convinced that he was listening; that he was watching after me from heaven.

“I had to. To keep you and your mother safe.”

"*Safe*?" I spit out, my fingers curling around the back of the armchair. "Safe?" I scream as I push the armchair to its side before approaching him.

"You lied. All of these years, you *lied* to me! You *lied* to mom!"

"I did *not* lie to your mother, Sofia! She knew the cost of being with me. I tried to change for her, but I couldn't change who I was! I gave her a choice!"

I blink several times as I stare up into his eyes. "What are you saying?"

He sighs and hangs his head before tucking his hands deep into the pockets of his suitcoat. "She knew. She knew that I wasn't dead. When my father died, it was time for me to take his place. I would have deceived my family if I did not. When it was time for me to go, she gave me an ultimatum—I either stay, or I never see you or her again."

I lick my lips as my gaze drifts to the window. She knew the entire time.

"I didn't want to leave you, Sofia. There would have been bloodshed if I would have stayed. Your brother was only ten. They would have killed him along with the rest of my blood. I was sure that Lidiya would have kept you safe. She was a good mother. She loved you more than anything in the world."

I look over his shoulder and frown at Alexei … my *brother*.

"How is it that I have an older brother? Mom said that I was an only child," I whisper, though I'm not sure if I want to hear the answer.

"Alexei was born six years before you. He's your half-brother. His mother died during child birth."

I place my fingers on my temples in an attempt to alleviate the headache that's crept up on me. My father reaches out and takes a step towards me.

I step back. "I want you to leave," I growl as I narrow my eyes at him.

His hand drops to his side as he purses his lips. "Sofia—"

"Get out!" I shriek, causing him to back away. "Stick to your promise, *Papa*! You had the option! You've made your bed, now you have to lie in it."

I shove my way past a group of men as I go searching for Dimitri. My chest heaves as rage courses throughout my body. I'm seeing red. I'm not hurt, I'm *livid.*

Once I reach the door of Dimitri's office—the place where he houses dead animals—I turn the knob and swing open the door.

He's meeting with another man, but stops when he sees me. Dimitri nods for the man to leave, and I move out of the way to let him before slamming the door shut and approaching my husband.

I slowly walk toward him with my fists balled at my sides. I want to scream. I want to yell, but I have to be cautious with Dimitri. Things have been going well, regardless of the circumstances. When he married me, I practically became royalty. He has even regarded me differently. Still, I don't know if I can reel myself in if he tells me what I think he will … *what I hope he won't.*

He watches me as I approach his desk and sit in the chair across from him. His amber eyes dance like fire as they survey me. It's an unspoken challenge.

Know your place, Sofia, or he'll remind you.

"How long did you know?" I whisper, my fingers tightening around the armrests of the sleek, leather chair.

He leans back in his chair as his eyes remain locked onto mine from across the desk. "The entire time," he says, nonchalantly.

My chest collapses as a long, rough breath tumbles from my lips. To be frank, I should know better. I shouldn't expect anything good from this man, yet I can't keep the disappointment from creeping into my mind and my heart.

"You knew that he was alive, yet you allowed me to believe that he was *dead*?"

He nods, his stoic expression remains unchanged.

"Why was I made to marry you?"

He shrugs. "To secure an alliance."

"An alliance?"

Dimitri leans forward and places his elbows on the desk. "Between my family and yours."

My eyes travel to my lap as I slowly shake my head. *Well, there you have it Sofia*. The Dmitriev name is tainted. My family is no better than the Vavilovs.

"My family, they're in the mafia?"

"They are," he says as he stands and walks around the desk. He leans against it and stares down at me as he grips the edge. "The Vavilovs and Dmitrievs have been feuding for decades. Vadim didn't know who you were when he took you. I am afraid that was a matter of *fate … destiny* if you will. He didn't know who that crazy old man was either when he shot him in the head. We only found out who you were when we found this. You had it in your pocket when Vadim took you."

Dimitri hands me a folded piece of paper, and I automatically know what it is.

"She left me with so many lies," I whisper as I stare down at her letter. "She wanted me to come here. Why? Why would she want this for me?"

He kneels down and places his hands on my cheeks. "Appreciate that I found you, Sofia. Appreciate that I *saved* you. Your father, he abandoned you—but me? I will never leave."

My blades cut through the ice as I glide aimlessly around my personal rink. I don't have the drive anymore. My will is lost. My heart is hollow, and my soul is bruised … my mind riddled with questions that I know I'll never get the answers to.

The person that I looked up to most in life, the person that I trusted more than any other … she lied, and I can't even ask her why. She died with her secrets, leaving me with her façade.

I collapse to my knees in the center of the rink and allow the tears to fall. My life was nothing but a travesty. The tears are seemingly the old me escaping from my tainted soul, dripping from my chin and landing onto the ice below. That's where the old me belongs, not the new me. Not anymore.

Nothing would be more of an injustice to my mother like giving up my dream, and that's exactly what I plan on doing. I do not owe her my success. Not after what she did.

I clench my teeth and pull at my hair as a growl escapes me.

Once I'm sure that my tear ducts have shriveled up from overuse, a raspy breath escapes me. My eyes travel to the window across the way, and I see Boris. His eyebrows pinch together as he looks at me gravely.

My lips part when two arms wrap around me and a stubbly cheek presses against mine. I look at Vadim's silhouette through bleary eyes as he holds me close. I relax into his embrace, the ice cold beneath me as his chest rises and falls against my back.

"Do *not* become a ghost, Sofia. Do *not* fall apart."

His words ignite more tears to form, and when my eyes travel back to the window, Boris is gone.

"It's too late," I whisper as I stare blankly at the window, and his arms tighten around my shoulders.

"I'm already a ghost."

Chapter 25

Every Family has its Black Sheep

DIMITRI

Several Weeks Later…

"How much longer does he have?" I ask.

My father's vrach looks up as he packs his stethoscope into his briefcase. "He's teetering the fine line between life and death. I'd say a couple of hours … maybe a day. When he does go, he will go peacefully."

I nod as I press my knuckles to my lips. The doctor leaves, and I stand, approaching my father's bedside.

Over the past couple of weeks, I've watched my father deteriorate. One day, he laid down to take a nap and he never got back up. His old body had finally called it quits. Sitting beside him, my eyes travel over his withered face. Deep wrinkles surround his eyes and slither down his cheeks. His eyes are closed and his chest rises slightly with each shallow breath.

"You thought that I was oblivious," I murmur as I stare down at him. "You thought that I didn't know what you did to her."

A smile curls my lips momentarily when I think of my sweet mother, but my face drops into a frown as the dark memory slinks its way into my mind.

"Please don't do this!" My mother wailed as I peered through the crack in their bedroom door.

He held her by her neck as he glared at her. "You are a whore!"

Her heavy breaths soon turned into a strangled sound as he lifted her by her neck. She kicked and struggled, but mama was only four-foot-something and no match against a man of my father's stature.

"You've made your choice, Vera. Now you must pay the price."

Reaching across my father's lifeless body, I retrieve a pillow and clutch it in my fists as I stare down at him.

"Mama was a good woman, and you killed her. You strangled the life out of her. She was the only person who's ever loved me."

My face twists as my fingers tighten around the pillow. "What did I ever get from you, old man? Nothing. Not a fucking thing."

Leaning forward, I watch as his lips part slightly, as if he is trying to speak. "You know what?" I whisper, "I get the last laugh."

I shove the pillow over his face and smile wickedly has his body seizes up. After several seconds, he's gone.

Just like that.

Standing, I place the pillow back into its respected place as my father's dead eyes stare up at the ceiling.

The doctor was wrong. A man like my father doesn't deserve to go peacefully. I assume the same will be said about me when it's my time.

Once I emerge from my father's room, I see Vlad. I don't try to hide my smile as I approach the big oaf.

"Call the artist. It's time to hang my painting in its rightful place."

His eyes flit from me to my father's bedroom door as a concerned expression spreads over his face.

"*Now*."

He nods slowly before continuing down the opposite direction of the hall, and I go searching for Sofia.

Once I enter the library, it takes Sofia and Vadim a moment to realize that I'm standing in the doorway. Sofia is sitting in a chair with her feet propped up on the desk that Vadim leans on. They're laughing and carrying on. The smile on her face is one that I've never seen her wear before. It's free and legitimate. Not forced … not *fake*.

I clear my throat as I enter the room and Vadim's eyes lazily travel up to meet mine.

"Vadim, arrangements need to be made. My father is dead."

A pained look crosses his face for a split second before his features harden once more as he stands straight, hurriedly leaving Sofia and me alone. I close the door behind him and approach her.

"Hello, beautiful," I whisper as I sweep her soft, blonde locks away from her face. "You are no longer a princess, but a queen. Extravagant vacations, the finest jewels … I'm going to give you the world."

I lean over the back of the chair where she sits and kiss her softly along the crook of her neck causing her to sigh. "I need you to become invested in the business, mouse."

"What do you need me to do?" She breathes out as I run my tongue along her jaw.

I stand straight and begin slowly massaging her shoulders. "It isn't what I *need* you to do, Sofia. It's what I *want* you to do."

Walking around the desk, I lean against the sturdy wood and stare into her dark, disconnected eyes. "Me being a young successor, I'm going to have other bratva's coming at me from every angle. I need to know that my wife will stay by my side every step of the way."

"Just tell me what you want, Dimitri," she snaps.

I tilt my head as I regard her sudden attitude. "An attitude will get you nowhere, mouse. You are the ship, and I am the sails. When I ask for your cooperation, it is recommended that you smile and do as I wish. Otherwise, you will not like the consequences."

She sighs and stares down at her lap and I straighten my spine. "The videos have become very popular as of late, but I don't wish to stop there. I have other plans, and I need you to help me."

"Help you?" she rasps, her eyes travelling to mine.

"Yes," I respond sharply. "Help me. There is a new thriving market for taboo films. Snuff is still in high demand, but we need to spread our clientele. We do that by meeting different needs."

I push off of the desk and place a finger under her chin. "I want you to be my star, Sofia. I want you to be the one that other men long for, but cannot have."

She shakes her head slowly, her eyes shimmering. "I can't, Dimitri. Please. Please don't make me do this."

I nod as a smile tugs at my lips. "You will. You will because you are my wife. You will, because you do not have a choice." I remove my finger from her chin and her head drops down as I continue. "You *will*, because you are *mine*."

Her lip trembles as her soft, brown eyes stare into mine. "I can't kill people."

I laugh. "Kill people? You won't be killing anyone, mouse, but you will be using them. For my gain, and for yours." She frowns. "There is no denying the rush that I get when I know that I have full control over a person. I want you to feel that, too."

She lets out a defeated sigh and shakes her head. "What exactly do you want me to do?"

I reach down and grasp her hand, pulling her to her feet. Reaching out, I gently run a finger from her cheekbone to her jaw.

"First, I want you to watch."

I lead her down below the dacha's polished floors. Her thin fingers tighten around my hand as she stops abruptly. I look over my shoulder and give her a tug, causing her feet to pick up once more.

"I remember this," she murmurs as her eyes travel to the openings on each side of the corridor. Some of the arched doorways are covered with a red curtain, and some have the curtain drawn to the side.

"Oh?" I say, leading her into one of the open rooms and releasing her hand. She nods slowly as her eyes travel around, her hands rub up and down her arms in an attempt to warm them.

"It's so cold," she whispers as she continues to take in her surroundings.

Each room that lines the corridor is pure concrete, and that only traps the chill in the air. There aren't any furnaces or fireplaces down here to offer solace from the cold, and I prefer it that way. The cold keeps the women on their toes, and it makes the blows hurt much worse.

I nod to a cage situated in the corner. "Get in."

Her eyes dart to the metal cage and she shakes her head emphatically. "No. I can't go back in there."

I begin approaching her with narrowed eyes. "Did I stutter, or did you misunderstand our little chat earlier?" Reaching behind her, my hand slides over the nape of her neck before I tangle my fingers in her hair. "Get. In. Now."

She sucks in a breath as my grip tightens in her hair and I pull her to the cage. I toss her inside, and she winces when her back hits the metal bars. I slam the door shut and smirk at her.

"Don't tell me no again, Sofia. In fact, you might as well remove that word from your vocabulary."

She hangs her head, and I turn when I hear footsteps approaching the entrance. Vlad drags in one of the newer whores, though we've already become acquainted—several times. Her wide, blue eyes dart around before locking onto Sofia, then her gaze softens when it lands on me.

I grip the whore's arm before dragging her to the center of the room. Her name is irrelevant; she's merely a fuck toy, but Sofia doesn't need to know that. Turning towards Sofia, I run a hand over the young woman's front. She only wears scraps of clothing; some leather shorts and a waist corset. Her breasts are uncovered, and I grasp her breast before twisting her nipple. She cries out, and Sofia's brow pinches together as she watches.

"Do you like that, slave? Do you like the pain that I give you?" My eyes never leave Sofia's when I whisper the question to the whore.

Sofia is fighting something within herself, it's written all over her face. One emotion transitions into another as she fights her feelings of jealously. The confusion glistens in her eyes as she grips the bars of the cage, her knuckles turning white.

I can see her thoughts. *"Should I be upset? Should I be angry?" Yes, no, yes, no* ... She is the epitome of beauty when she battles with herself. It makes my cock press painfully against my fly as I watch my beautiful wife come undone against her will. Her thoughts no longer belong to her, they belong to me and only me.

I grasp the woman's hair and pull her head back to expose her neck before biting into her flesh. She tenses up in my arms, and I sigh as my teeth cut into the sensitive skin. I pull away and blow on the indents left behind.

"Shhh…"

She loosens up in my arms and I lift her hands above her head before cuffing her wrists. This isn't our first powwow. I've been conditioning this one for weeks. She relishes in the pain … she wants it. Something that Sofia will soon learn.

Sofia watches me like a hawk when I walk across the room and pull the rope, lifting the girl to where her toes can barely touch the cold floor below. I grab the bamboo cane and circle around the whore, feeling the burn from Sofia's dagger eyes. She can hate me all she wants. The fact of the matter is, she doesn't hate me for what I'm about to do to this woman—she hates me because it isn't her, whether she wants to admit it or not.

I walk toward the hanging girl as the cane swings casually by my side. "Do you know the beauty of mixing pain with pleasure, Sofia? Most will never comprehend the beauty of the two together." I stand in front of the woman, rearing back and landing the cane over the goosebumps that have spread over her breasts. She tenses up before her chin falls to her chest. "But the reality is, it's a primal need." I look over my shoulder into Sofia's questioning eyes. "When you see two animals fuck, what do they do? Generally, the female lays on her belly while the male uses her for one thing. Her job is to grow babies in her womb, but his, *his* job is to spread his seed. *His* job is to dominate. To *own*. He bites her, pins her down, takes what he wants. It is no different with man. We are the dominant of the two sexes."

She shakes her head and diverts her eyes.

"Just like you, mouse. When you first came here and I locked onto you, you nearly let me have you without ever speaking a word to me."

"I didn't," she grits out, her eyes latching onto mine once more. "I *didn't* let you have me. You took what you wanted."

"You would have eventually. If you're going to sit here and feed me a bunch of moralistic garbage, I guess you need to take the slave's place, don't you? You can sit there and pretend that this doesn't bother you, but the reality is that it does. Come off of your high-horse. Quit pretending that you do not like it when I touch you … when I *fuck* you—"

"And what if it does?" she spits out. "It wouldn't change a fucking thing, Dimitri."

I smile at her admission, because that's basically what it was. Sofia is too proud to spit out the truth plain as day. She loves to play on words.

"You're right, mouse. It wouldn't change a *fucking* thing."

I turn towards the brunette woman and lay the cane across her chest once more, causing her to shriek. I continue beating the woman until the bright red marks have crisscrossed every single inch of her exposed flesh. Her chin brushes against her chest as she slumps down, her toes still grazing the floor below. Sofia remains in the cage, arms crossed over her chest as she glares at me.

I'm no longer cold as the adrenaline pumps through my veins. Beads of sweat cover my entire body as I circle the slave. "Pick your face up," I snap, and her bright blue eyes find mine. "Tell me that you want to suck me … that you want to swallow my come."

She nods and does as she's told. "I want to swallow your come, master," she whispers, and I whip her thigh with the cane.

"*Louder*!"

"I want to swallow your come! Please, fuck my mouth!"

I smile as I reach above her head and remove the cuffs, allowing her to fall to the floor. I place my hands on the back of my head as she undoes my button and fly, freeing my cock. I take no time as I shove my length down her throat, holding her there as the gagging sounds echo throughout the room. "Keep me there," I growl as I remove my hands.

She does as she's told, keeping my full length inside of her warm mouth as tears stream down her cheeks and drool dribbles over her chin.

"Now," I murmur, and she removes me from her mouth, gripping my cock in one hand and stroking me as she catches her breath. "Take me back into your mouth."

She nods and instantly begins fucking me with her mouth. Her movements are quick. She's eager to please. My own needs are of more importance than hers, and that's how it should be. That is how these relationships are constructed. They are not built on love or trust; they are built on my needs.

My eyes lock onto Sofia's as she watches me. Her gaze is impassive. I'm sure she feels sorrow for this girl. Well, she needs to get over that. However, when I look into those brown eyes, my dick becomes soft in the whore's mouth. It isn't this woman that I want, the one that I want is in the cage, and her stoic eyes haunt me. They remind me of our two bodies and their capabilities.

I push the whore away and she gasps. "Go."

She nods hastily and jumps to her feet, a pained look spreading across her face as she escapes the room. Vlad is waiting for her right outside of the curtain. He'll take her back to the chamber where we house the shlyukhi before they are sold to the highest bidder.

"Well?" I whisper as I approach the cage.

She cocks her head to the side. "Well, what, Dimitri? You brought me down here to show me a woman sucking your cock after you beat her with a cane? What was the point? You're showing me because you want it to be me hanging from the rafters? You want to beat me with a cane? You want to force your dick down my throat and make me gag on it?"

I sneer at her. “You are becoming quite the little brave one, mouse.”

Her lips curl up as she looks at me with mock admiration. “I’m sorry, let me start over. That display was absolutely captivating, how you kept her from biting your dick off is beyond me—”

“Enough!” I holler, but she continues.

“You are an exceptional master. You’ve warped that woman’s mind, and you’ve done your job, right? That is what you brought me down here to see, no?”

I kneel down in front of the cage and stare into her eyes. “What has gotten into you?”

She shakes her head slowly as a trembling breath escapes her lips. “You married me, whether or not I wanted it, I didn’t have a choice … not one,” she whispers, tears filling her eyes. “Now, you remind me again that it was only for one reason. Not that you wanted me, but to use me as a tool to get what you wanted. I’m nothing to you, and you’ve reminded me of that time and time again. Though, I should thank you. I should thank you for never allowing me to care about you … to fall in love with you.”

I frown as I watch the tears spill from her eyes. She’s never opened up to me; she’s never been honest until now. Honesty is a dangerous thing, but even as my fists tighten, I can't be angry at her admission.

"You never would have fallen for a man like me, Sofia. It wouldn't matter if I didn't take you. Regardless of what you believe, I didn't know who you were when you were brought into my home … when I stopped the inevitable from happening to you."

She hastily wipes the tears from her cheeks—they're evidence of her hurt, and she doesn't want to give that to me. "Please let me out of here."

Chapter 26

Silence Invokes Violence

SOFIA

I keep my lips pursed as Dimitri follows me up the stairs to his bedroom. I cracked. I swore that I wouldn't allow him to see that. Up until that moment, I had kept my true feelings under lock and key for fear that my words wouldn't go unpunished. Now, after his response, my fear is even greater.

He opened up, *too*.

Dimitri is utterly terrifying, but he's also incredibly enigmatic. Malevolence wrapped in a beautiful package—that is Dimitri. I have kept my questions from slipping, because I didn't want to allow him to sway my opinion of what he is: a monster. I also didn't want to become a statistic: a woman who fell madly in love with her captor.

Like settled dust, it didn't take much for him to stir up the many questions, causing them to swirl waywardly in my mind. All it took was for him to breathe a little truth to make me question *everything*.

I sigh as I reach for the doorknob, but I freeze when his chest presses against my back.

"I want you to understand," he whispers against my shoulder.

"There isn't anything to understand, Dimitri. I will do what you want, and I'll do it solely to survive," I say, turning the doorknob and pushing the door open.

I step into the room, and he stays on my heels as he follows me inside. I'm not sure what he thinks he's going to gain out of all of this. He already has me under his thumb, which means that his alliance has been secured with my father. Now, it seems that every one of his actions regarding me are merely for his entertainment.

This man isn't capable of caring. The fact that he's trying to convince me that he does is nothing more than a cruel joke. When I was in the cage earlier, his eyes were convincing. They showed remorse, even humanity for a split second. I suppose even the cruelest can feel for their victims.

Dimitri wraps his fingers around my arms and squeezes them gently. "You may not love me, Sofia, but

I do have feelings for you. Perhaps it is love, but how am I to know? How am I to know what *this* is?"

My lips curl into a sad smile. "I know about love, Dimitri. You don't love me. You don't care for me. You simply want to own me … control me … render me soulless. That isn't love. Love is beautiful. It isn't pinning down someone's wings—it's setting them free."

His fingers tighten around my arms momentarily, but then he releases me and walks to the bathroom. I change into some cozy pajama pants and a tank top before climbing into bed. I curl up and watch the flames lick the top of the fireplace as Dimitri showers.

I slide my hand over my stomach and sigh when I think of the tiny speck that's steadily growing in my womb. For a man that watches my every move, it's surprising that he failed to realize that I had missed an entire period. Somehow, I was one of the small percentage of women who actually conceive while on birth control. The vrach has yet to check me out, but I can feel it. My body is changing.

When the door opens, my eyes follow his masculine form as he walks to the dresser with a towel wrapped around his waist. I would be lying if I said that I hated him or that I didn't have feelings for him, because I do.

Each time his front cracks open, I see a sincere man. A man that's probably been through a lot … a man that has a heart.

His constant change of demeanor is enough to give me whiplash. At times, I wonder if he'll be pushed far enough to the brink to end me once and for all. Yet, moments like these, I wonder if he'll change for the better. If I could get him to *love* me … to *cherish* me. Maybe a baby will do that. Maybe a child would be the stamp that would seal his madness out of our lives once and for all.

When he climbs into bed, he wraps an arm around my waist and pulls me to him. A chill shoots down my spine when he buries his nose in my hair.

"I am not every man, Sofia. I do not plan on allowing you to be free because you're mine. You're my wife. I have never wanted anything as much as I wanted you when I first looked into your eyes. For me, that was all that I needed. That was all that I needed to know that there was something very special in you. Pinning down your wings? Yes, and I'm afraid that will never stop, but *freeing* you? Absolutely not. I never said that I was not a selfish man, because I am. I may not know about love, mouse, but I know what you do to me."

“What are you saying?” I rasp, squeezing my eyes shut as I await his answer.

He rolls me onto my back, and his cognac eyes look straight through me. They show a softness that he displays to me rarely; when he cracks open his frigid heart to show me the valves that still pump occasionally—the piece of him that is human.

“I do love you, Sofia. In my own way, yes, but there is no denying my feelings for you.” His mouth snaps shut as he stares down into my questioning eyes. His eyebrows pull together when I remain silent. “Say something,” he whispers, circling his thumb over my cheek.

My lips part as I try and sort my thoughts. He said it. He loves me, but he doesn’t plan on that changing a thing. He doesn’t know me. He only knows the captive that I’ve become. What would he think of the real Sofia Dmitriev? The one that was driven. The one that never gave up. The one that chased her dreams and made them a reality.

His goal is to crush my aspirations—to render me useless and dependent until I see him as a god. He *likes* the idea of love. He *likes* the idea of marriage, but his ideologies are so incredibly skewed.

I watch in astonishment as his eyes morph; caring cognac irises turn into hard, hot burning embers as his pupils swell. Reaching up, I grab his face and press my lips to his. Silence invokes violence with Dimitri, but while I'm working up the nerve to spit out the words, perhaps a kiss will help him simmer down.

I pull away and look into his eyes. "I love you Dimitri."

I lie, yet the smooth words that roll off my tongue are convincing enough to cause a slight smile to curl his lips.

A hard body against soft, female curves. Slow movements, soft kisses, and whispered words. As Dimitri makes love to me, it's hard to overrule his declaration. Not one inch of skin has gone uncherished. Not one kiss has been meaningless. Every now and then, I'll allow my eyes to flutter open to see him staring down at me with his bottom lip clamped between his teeth.

His gaze is true and unsettling.

I can't see anybody else … I can't think of anything else.

All I know is him—and once more, the lie that tumbled from my lips drifts further, and further to the truth each time I whisper, *"I love you."*

"You have not been skating," Vadim states as I stare out the window.

The month is May, yet snow still clings to the tree branches. It doesn't look much different out there than it did in the middle of winter.

"When does the snow melt?"

"A heat wave is expected later this week, but I'm afraid if you're looking for warmth, you will not find it here. The average temperature during summer is around thirty degrees."

I sigh. "So basically this place is a cold, bottomless pit."

Vadim laughs. "Well, considering what you're used to in America—yes. You could say that."

My stomach lurches and I place my fingers over my lips. Vadim rushes to my side. "What is it?"

I shake my head. "It's nothing. I haven't been feeling well."

"How long have you been feeling unwell? You were fine yesterday."

My eyes travel to his. "I need your help."

Vadim shakes his head slowly. "It depends on what you need, krasavaya."

I swallow hard as I look into his eyes intently, working up the courage to spit the words out. "Vadim, I'm pregnant. I haven't told Dimitri. I need you to somehow take me to a doctor."

His eyes grow wide as my secret soaks in. "Why would you need me to take you to a doctor? And why have you not told Dimitri? The vrach that he hired for you is one of the best. She will ensure that you have a healthy pregnancy."

I shake my head slowly, and his wide eyes sober as he practically reads my mind. "Sofia, are you asking me to help you terminate this pregnancy?"

I huff as my gaze falls to my lap. "I cannot consciously bring a child into this life, Vadim. It would be wrong."

Vadim walks away from me and stares out the window, placing his hands on top of his head. "I cannot, Sofia. I *will not*."

“It’s the least you could do!” I snap, glaring at his back. “Can I have at least one choice? If I can do anything for this unborn child, I would save him or her the heartbreak.”

“You intend on murdering your husband’s child without uttering a word to him about it? Sofia, I have come to know you well, and the girl that I know would never consider doing something like this. I refuse to help you.”

I leap up and ball my fists at my sides. “I’ve never asked you for anything. Not once. Considering what you’ve done, Vadim—you owe me your life seeing as you’ve ripped mine to shreds.”

He whips around and shoots daggers at me. “Do you not think that I suffer every day? Do you not think that I’ve thought of a million ways to turn back time?” He takes several steps towards me. “Do you think that I wouldn’t have taken you for myself? That I wouldn’t have claimed you before he did?”

I sigh as his lips hover inches from mine. “You could have, but you didn’t. You killed my uncle, drugged me, and then threw me in a cage. You sprayed me down and left me in a puddle of freezing water and tears. You barely fed me. You had every intention of dragging me into a room and having me brutally raped and murdered for someone's viewing pleasure."

His eyes flutter shut as I lean forward and brush my lips against his. "I wanted you to touch me. I wanted you *there*, but you stopped. Even after everything, I needed your touch more than anything. You refused me, and now you're refusing me again."

"If I could, I would. But I can't. If we're caught, he'd kill us both."

"So that's it," I whisper, stepping away.

Vadim tilts his head as he looks at me solemnly. "That night, when you slid my hand between your thighs, you were confused. You didn't know what you wanted. You were afraid, and you still are afraid—but eventually, you will learn that I'm not your hero. I cannot be your hero. I am a Vavilov, and you are too. You need to accept what is. You are family, and now you are to give birth to the Pakhan's child. Dimitri will continue to treat you well if you continue to keep him happy. Don't do something that will change that."

I shake my head. "You're wrong. I didn't put your hand on my pussy because I was afraid. I did it because I wanted you." Running my hand through my hair, I look into his keen eyes. "Dimitri is leaving in several days to go to the Ukraine. If you change your mind, please let me know."

Chapter 27

Actions Speak Louder

VADIM

I crave her. Her lips, her skin … her absolute determination. Even now, with Dimitri's child growing inside of her—I want her. More than anything, I wish that I could help her, but that's impossible. Even if I did decide to take her, there are guards swarming the dacha and standing guard around the perimeter.

When she first came here, I didn't care. She was a product. Nothing more than flesh and bone, but then I discovered her soul. I discovered that there was an inner beauty that matched the exterior.

As I stand before the door, my heart threatens to beat through my chest. I want her to know that she's thawed my icy heart; a heart that's been frozen from the inside out ever since that fateful day. What I never conceived was that a life of crime would eventually seep over onto the ones that I held closest to my heart—my wife and my *child*.

When Sasha died, Galina did too. I never wanted to admit that I was the root cause of her death. Sasha was only twelve years old and, when a business deal went bad, she became a lesson. One that I will never forget.

She was raped and left for dead on the shore of The Black Sea. Her coal black hair surrounded her sweet face like a halo and her eyes were shut. I was at least grateful for that. I don't know how I would live with myself if I had to look into her lifeless, dead eyes.

Galina was never the same, but I wasn't either. She turned to a life of drugs, and I traded my existence for a life of apathy. I not only failed my daughter, but I failed my wife, too. When she left, I didn't utter a word … I didn't ask her to stay. I wanted to forget about those happy times. I wanted to forget about *everything*.

I open the door and peer inside.

Sofia sits on the bed as she stares at the fire. Her long, blonde hair hangs over her shoulder, and the robe that she wears is practically see-through. I can see her beautiful round breasts through the fabric.

I clear my throat and her soft eyes travel to mine.

"Vadim," she whispers as she stands.

I take note of her wobbly legs as she leans on the bed for support. She appears drunk.

"Sofia," I growl as I enter the room, quickly closing the door behind me. "Have you been drinking?"

She giggles as her feet drag against the floor. "I thought that I'd have a couple of drinks. What's wrong with that?" she slurs, falling into my arms. Her brown eyes latch onto mine. "I was hoping that you'd come for me. I want you."

"It is foolish for you to drink Sofia, and you know why."

She lazily presses a finger to my lips. "I don't want to talk about that. I want you to take me to the bed, and *fuck* me."

Sofia lowers herself to her knees before me, clumsily unbuckling my belt before unzipping my pants.

"What are you doing?" I rasp as she pulls my dick out and begins running her hand up and down my shaft. She smiles at me deviously before her lips part and she takes me into her mouth. I sigh as she slowly works her way up and down, her eyes never leaving mine.

"Stop it," I murmur, causing her lips to curl up as she sucks me. "Stop. Now!" I sneer, grasping her arms and pulling her to her feet. I back her to the bed, grasping her waist and sitting her down on the edge of the mattress. "What are you doing?"

Sofia reaches in front of her and pulls at the belt of the robe. When she pulls the robe open, I suck in a breath. Her beautiful body is bare before me as she rocks back and forth with her legs spread wide, welcoming me. Her pussy is glistening from her desire and my hard cock is merely inches away, aching to be inside of her.

Her gaze remains locked onto my pained face as I stare down at her opening, wanting nothing more than to have her—to use her to quiet the voices of the past—but the feasible part of my mind screams in resistance.

This is your cousin's, the Pakhan's, wife. She is pregnant with his child.

I reach forward and grasp her jaw, pulling her face close to mine. "You are treading in dangerous waters. Who is to say that I will not tell Dimitri of your transgressions? That you *tried* and *failed* to fuck his own cousin?"

"That's where you're wrong Vadim," she whispers, reaching between us and grasping my length before running the head of my cock along her slit. "I won't fail. You want this as much as I do."

I allow my hand to loosen around her neck as I look into her eyes. "You're drunk. Tomorrow, meet me in the library. The usual time."

I turn, tucking my throbbing length back into my pants and walk towards the door.

"You can't keep leaving me like this Vadim," Sofia seethes, making me stop in my tracks.

I look over my shoulder into her hurt face. I'm disappointing her, and tomorrow it won't be any better I'm afraid.

"Go to sleep, krasavaya," I whisper, continuing on my way out the door. Once it's closed, a blunt object hits the wood followed by her scream.

Tucking my hands in my pockets, I sigh as I walk down the narrow hallway to my bedroom.

As I sit in the library, I check the old clock that hangs from the wall every few minutes. She's late … or she's just decided not to come. She's either embarrassed or pissed; maybe both. She doesn't hide her stubbornness from me like she does with Dimitri. Then again, he scares the shit out of her.

He scares the shit out of me.

When he was younger, I would put a swift boot to his ass and he'd listen. When he began getting older, I started becoming concerned. His father always thought that there was something wrong with the boy, and he was right to worry.

A fight between the two of us would be a good one; he's strong, and I am too. He frightens me because he holds the fate of this family in his grasp. I could try to overthrow him, but what would that do? His painting has yet to be completed and hung in the hallway, yet his tyrannical rule lingers in the air—it's suffocating. I'd always hoped that his fucked up determination would end up being a good thing. That it would frighten our enemies and keep us ahead of the race. However, he lacks something that his father had: a level head.

Now he's got our biggest rival's daughter under his thumb. Not only that, he's obsessed with her. I am too. I'm afraid that it's only a matter of time before I snap … when he hurts her again, I can't see myself being able to stand by and watch it happen.

I hear commotion outside and walk to the window. Looking out, I smile as I watch Sofia yank her arm from Boris' grip as she stomps to the frozen lake. He hangs his shoulders, defeated. He likes her. I could tell when I first saw him go to her that night.

She pulls the skates on, forcefully yanking the laces before tying them. Then, she's off; soaring over the ice and holding her arms out like the beautiful swan that she is. I'm entranced, and my eyes never leave her—not even when I hear the ice crack, or when the lake opens up and swallows her whole.

"*Sofia*!"

I keep hearing her name being shouted, and I realize that it's me hollering frantically as my feet pound against the hard wood.

Chapter 28

Icy Heart

VADIM

When I reached the lake, I thought that I'd already lost her. Below the surface of the slushy water, my eyes locked onto hers as the tiny bubbles rose to the surface. I didn't think twice when I dove in for her.

I ignored the overwhelming sensation of being frozen alive as the precious seconds ticked by. I didn't have long until hypothermia claimed us both, yet I wasn't concerned about my well-being. I couldn't allow another to die at my hands. I've cheated death dozens of times, but I couldn't allow her to slip through my fingers.

I kicked frantically, chasing her into the darkness as she descended further into the depths of the lake. Once I reached her, I held her close as I kicked back to the surface, hoping and praying that she wasn't lost to the one thing that she loved like no other.

We coughed in unison once we emerged from the water. Boris helped pull her out before grasping my forearm and dragging me across the ice. The cold air breathed across my flesh, and it stung like nothing I've ever felt before.

I ignored my excessive shivering. It seemed like my own lungs had begun to succumb to the chill as my body worked feverishly to function. I carried her small, frozen form back to the dacha refusing to look at her. I was *angry*. I was angry because I was afraid. If she died, so help me I would end myself.

Once I got her inside, I laid her on the couch in the study before stripping her out of her clothes. Her skin was raised with goosebumps as I demanded that Boris retrieve blankets, towels—anything to wrap her in. He stood there like a statue, his face ghost white as he stared at her naked form.

"*Now*!" I snapped, causing him to jump into action.

Once I wrapped the blankets around her, I stripped out of my own clothes, stopping every now and then to rub my hands up and down her body. Her lips were blue and her skin was the palest I've ever seen it, but she was breathing; her heart was still beating. She was *alive*.

I held her close until her body loosened up in my arms and her profuse shivering began to die down as she warmed up.

I sit in the darkness of the foyer as the smoke from my cigarette swirls before drifting toward the ceiling. I take another swig from the bottle as the door nearly splinters open. Dimitri's eyes go traveling before they snap to me.

"What the fuck, Vadim? Tell me she's okay, or so help me God I will have your head on a platter."

I smirk before taking a drag. "A head on a platter? That should be in one of your videos, cousin."

He eyes me momentarily before his gaze travels to the stairs. "Tell me that my wife is alive."

I sigh as I place the bottle beside me and stand. "She's alive. It was a close call."

Approaching him, I snuff my cigarette out in the standing ashtray. "You act concerned, but I wonder if it's due to her well-being or for your alliance with the Dmitrievs."

His eyes snap to mine. "*Both*. Believe it or not, I care for her."

I laugh as I run a hand down my face. "Well, I suppose that's good to know."

"What are you getting at?" he sneers, narrowing his eyes.

I shrug and he takes a step toward me.

"Cousin, I would recommend that you learn your place. You are my council now per my father's wish, but don't think for a second that that will not change. I thank you for going to her and stopping the inevitable from happening, but watch your tongue when it comes to me and my *wife*."

I clamp my teeth together as I stare into his crazed eyes. If only I could speak the truth, tell the asshole everything that he needs to hear, but I won't. I'll bite my tongue, and I'll continue to do so until I can come up with a plan. One that involves two people—not three.

Chapter 29

Life Goes On

SOFIA

It's a peaceful place below the ice. There, my life flashed before my eyes … memories. More good than bad. Those memories are all that I have left. I wanted the cold to claim me. Yet again, my choices were stolen from my grasp.

I'd underestimated myself long ago—when I swore that I'd never consider taking my own life. I didn't know how unrelenting life could really be. Suicide wasn't an option when my life was ripe with happiness. When that happiness was suddenly removed, disdain became my existence.

The fight left me once the ice cracked. It didn't take long for my supposed destiny to convince me. The fear that I've been plagued with left me when the lake swallowed me. The tunnel of light held me as the freezing water carried me below. The memories flickered like an old film as the cracked hole that pulled me under drifted farther and farther away.

I didn't fight it. I didn't want to. I didn't run a razor over my wrists or press the barrel of a gun to my temple, but not fighting for life is one in the same. I craved death and the closer that it got, I embraced it.

Vadim did me no favors when he dove in and saved me. He was only prolonging the torture. He was selfish in doing that. If he cared, he would have let me be.

My skin has thawed out for the most part. Vadim situated me in a large, cozy chair in front of the fire. He reassured me that Dimitri would be home soon. I don't know if he actually thought that was supposed to comfort me. Dimitri has already killed me a thousand times. If he wants a soulless robot, then he's doing a good job of creating one.

The idea of continuing to live this hell is brutal. I thought that I was finally being called home when the ice cracked below my feet, and I'd accepted it. I came to peace with saying goodbye to the cruel world that I've come to know.

The bedroom door cracks open, but I don't bother looking. My eyes stay trained on the dancing fire as it crackles, and I hear Dimitri's heavy breaths by the doorway where he stands.

"Sofia?" he croaks.

I frown at the pain in his tone. No, he can pretend to care … to love me, but the reality is plain as day. He's sick, and I'm the one that he wants to heal him.

I can't heal anyone when I, myself, am broken into a million tiny fragments.

His footsteps are hurried as he approaches and drops to his knees in front of me. Leaning forward, his bloodshot eyes glisten as he runs his fingers over my cheek. "Are you okay?" he rasps, the potent smell of vodka escaping his lips.

I stare blankly into his eyes as I nod my head slowly.

"Say something," he whispers as his eyes implore mine, but I can't.

My lips part, but I can't conjure up any words. They're just nonexistent.

"Sofia," he warns.

My lips snap shut. I'm emotionally and mentally spent. All that's happened over the past year is catching up. My fight is diminished—my soul is drained. I have nothing left to give. No words … no actions.

Dimitri places his hands on each side of my face and his eyes glimmer with that familiar anger that I've come to know well. He wants a *moment*. He wants my *words*, just like he wanted my *desire* … this man has taken everything from me, and he won't stop. He's relentless in that way.

I simply shake my head as my shoulders slump farther. I'm not tense because I'm not afraid anymore, and that angers my husband. More than anything, he wants my *fear.*

"Say. Something," he grits out, but again, I have nothing to say. His hands slip away from my face as his chest begins moving up and down rapidly from his hurried breaths. I can tell he is trying to control his madness, but he can't. Madness defines Dimitri. It isn't something that he can control.

When he rears back and strikes me across my face, I don't make a sound. Not one whimper … not one tear. When he picks me up and tosses me onto the bed, I allow it. I don't cower, and I don't fight. When he yanks my pants over my hips, I stare lifelessly at the ceiling.

When he slams into me with his length, my world spirals out of control. It's a reaction that I can't control.

Where Dimitri cannot control his madness towards me, the same can be said about my desire towards him.

He tangles his fingers in my hair as he stares into my lust drunk eyes. “See, mouse? We have something that cannot be ignored. You can try, and I know you do. But remember, *ty moy*.”

You are mine.

Dimitri hasn’t allowed me to leave his side.

I think he and Vadim are aware that I had tried to allow the icy depths to claim me. I haven’t been the same since that day. I barely eat or sleep. I’m depressed. My only friends are the shadows that dance across the walls waywardly as Dimitri sleeps beside me.

I stand at the window as Dimitri types away at his computer, twisting the intricately carved letter opener in my hands. He didn’t see me swipe it from his desk earlier. If he did, he would’ve taken it by now.

I consider doing the worst as I glance down at the letter opener. Attempting to kill myself wouldn’t do any good. Dimitri would stop it at once; putting me back together before I could wilt and die. But … the embryo that is steadily growing in my womb, I can save him or her.

Glancing over my shoulder, I see Dimitri is still busy working and my grip tightens around the handle of the letter opener. I cannot willingly bring a baby into this home. I cannot give Dimitri an heir to his sick, twisted throne. This decision wasn't a hard one to make, as sick as it may sound. Was it a painful decision to make? Most definitely, but it wasn't difficult to come to the realization that having a baby with this man isn't logical. I've gotten to this point—the point where shoving a letter opener into my womb is the only solution. Dimitri would be a cruel father, just like he's a cruel husband and person. A child wouldn't change a thing.

Squeezing my eyes shut, I position the pointed end of the letter opener above my womb. Taking in a breath, I say a little prayer for the child that I'll never know … but then, a knock sounds from the door, halting me.

I quickly turn and hide the letter opener behind my back as Dimitri says, "Yes?"

Vlad peers in through the door and eyes me momentarily before his gaze snaps to Dimitri. "Alexei Dmitriev is here to see Sofia."

Dimitri's lips curl into a devious smile. "Is that right? I'm sure that he does not have an appointment. Any visits between Sofia and the Dmitrievs are to go through me."

My heart picks up the pace when I see Alexei's soft brown eyes peer through the door behind Vlad. "I was in the area, and I wished to see my sister. I didn't realize that an appointment was necessary."

Dimitri glares at Alexei as he enters the office behind Vlad.

"You're a huntsman? We should get together sometime. I do love a good hunt," Alexei says, crossing his arms over his chest as he leans against the doorframe.

Dimitri smirks at him as he sits back in his chair. "How long do you need? We have a lunch date today with my sister and stepmother."

My brother shrugs. "Thirty minutes to an hour."

"I need her back by one o'clock sharp," Dimitri snaps.

Alexei nods. "As you wish."

I walk alongside Alexei silently as we make our way down the hall to the library. He's a handsome man, and he's much taller than me. He has our father's features, and I have my mother's, other than my father's blond hair. We do kind of look alike, though, and I find myself stealing glances at him.

Once we make our way into the library, I'm caught off guard when he swiftly shuts the door behind us and turns to face me. My shoulders curl in as he approaches me and places his hands on my cheeks.

"Has he been good to you, Sofia—and do *not* lie to me."

I stare up into his eyes, so much like my father's. "Would I be any safer with your mob, Alexei? The Dmitrievs are no better than the Vavilovs."

His eyes glimmer as he surveys my features … studying me … regarding me. "You know nothing of the Dmitrievs, sister. We are not heartless, and we are not brutes. These men … if you knew the half of it you would not have married Dimitri Vavilov."

I scoff at his statement. "You can't be serious. I didn't *choose* to marry him. I was taken. They killed my uncle—my mother's brother—and they took me. They were going to use me for one of their videos, but Dimitri decided to keep me for himself. I was forced to marry him to secure an alliance between our families, and now…." I pause, diverting my eyes.

"Now what, Sofia?" Alexei implores.

My eyes travel up to his as I swallow the lump in my throat. "I believe that I'm pregnant with his child."

Alexei releases me abruptly and takes a step back, running his fingers through his blond hair. "Are you certain?"

I nod. "I haven't seen a doctor, but I'm pretty certain."

"That bastard," he sneers as he begins pacing back and forth. "Papa and I … we thought that you married by choice. They sent us the video and you didn't seem to be in a state of despair."

My lips part as I think up a response, but Alexei's phone buzzes interrupting my thoughts.

"Da, Papa. YA s Sofiyey sikh por. YA budu na moyem puti v blizhaysheye vremya." He presses the button to end the call and his eyes snap to mine. "I need to go. I'll talk to Papa and see what needs to be done."

I reach out towards him as he approaches, before he wraps his arms around me in an embrace. Shockingly, it's comforting.

This is my *blood.*

This is my *brother.*

"What happens now?" I whisper against his shoulder, causing him to squeeze me tightly against his chest.

"You play the part, Sofia. You stay *alive*. At least until we can figure something out."

I heave one last time before wiping my mouth with the back of my hand.

"Are you alright?"

I startle at the sound of Dimitri's voice, and turn to face him after flushing the toilet. "Yes. I haven't been feeling well."

He cocks his head as he regards me. "You have not been feeling well for a while, Sofia. Is there something that you'd like to tell me?"

I twist my hands nervously in front of me. I'm still holding onto the hope that I can somehow terminate this pregnancy. Under different circumstances, I would never fathom an abortion—but these are not normal circumstances. I am a captive, and my husband is my captor. If I am to escape, a baby would make it all the more difficult.

"Mouse," he says as he steps closer and grasps my arms. "Are you with child? Are you to have my baby?"

I shake my head as I stare into his eyes. "I'm just not feeling well."

His jaw tenses, and his fingers tighten around my arms. "I'm afraid that your brother let the cat out of the bag. He thought that I already knew. Imagine my surprise at having that *idiot* disclose something that I should have been the first to know."

Tears fill my eyes as my gaze drops to his chest. "I'm sorry. I wasn't entirely sure. I was waiting for the vrach to come visit me. I was going to tell you when I was certain."

He sighs and his fingers loosen around my arms. "I've called the vrach, and she will be here shortly. Leaning down, he presses his lips to mine. "I wasn't ready for a child, mouse. But the thought of my child growing inside of you … I'm ready now. I'm ready to show you that I am more than capable of being the father that my father never was."

"Based on your last menstrual cycle, I'd say that you're three to four weeks. The pregnancy test was positive." The doctor smiles as she stands. "Congratulations."

Dimitri's smile actually reaches his eyes as he stares down at me. The same can't be said about me as I force a smile to spread across my face. I'm even more stuck than I was before, it seems. Now, I'll also have a baby to protect from this venomous man.

Once the doctor leaves, Dimitri lifts me into his arms. "We must tell the world, mouse. You are my queen, and now you are to have my prince."

5 Months Later

"How are you feeling?" Alina asks as we make our way through the garden.

It's the middle of summer, so it's warmer than usual. The garden is gargantuan, and the vegetables that grow feed us most of the time.

I sigh as I run my hand over my belly. "I'm okay. Tired most of the time, but okay. The baby is active. It never stops moving."

"And you are not sure of the sex, yet?"

I shake my head. "No, not yet. Dimitri wants to wait until the baby is born. He's convinced that it's a boy, but I have a feeling it's a little girl."

She chuckles. "Of course he thinks it's a boy. My brother is too proud. But you … you wish for a girl?"

My gaze snaps to hers. I hadn't really thought about what I want. At first, the terrifying realization of being pregnant was more than I could bare. It almost made me do the unthinkable, but now that this baby is growing inside of me … I can feel her. I think I already love her.

"Yeah. I guess I kind of do hope it's a girl."

She smiles. "Well, then I hope it's a girl too."

"Alina, do you think that your brother is ready for a child?"

She stops walking and I turn to face her. "I know that Dimitri isn't the easiest person, Sofia, but there are many reasons why he is the way that he is. You've softened him. I've never seen him care about anything until you. He would move mountains for you and that baby." She pauses as she continues walking, and I follow. "My father was always cruel to Dimitri. He killed our own mother, and Dimitri saw it all. Even after all of the beatings, he never changed until that moment."

I gasp. "The Pakhan? He murdered your mother?"

Alina nods. "He not only killed my mother, but he also killed a part of Dimitri; the part where he could love and show affection. That died with Mama. I know this doesn't mean much, Sofia, but you are reviving him. You are bringing out something that I've not seen since he was a little boy."

I blink several times. How I feel for Dimitri, it's from one extreme to the other. My emotions are like a pendulum; back and forth they swing. One moment I'm fulfilled, and the next I'm dangling by a string. I see what she's saying. I can also see little glimmers of hope when he kisses and talks to my belly … the sheer excitement in his eyes when he talks about becoming a father. However, that doesn't keep him from making his videos. It doesn't keep him from harming others. For now, it keeps him from harming me, but what is going to happen once the baby is born? Dimitri is only hesitant to strike me now because I'm with child. Eventually, he'll want me to partake in his perverse videos, and that alone makes my skin crawl. I can't do what he does. We're a different breed of person.

"You know, you are going to do well here if you please my brother. I can see the disdain in your eyes. I can see hatred too. You can hate my family all you want, but the fact is that you're now part of it."

My eyes snap to hers as I stop in my tracks. "I keep being told that it's up to me, but it isn't. Dimitri is a ticking time bomb. It takes nothing to anger him. What kind of world do you people live in to think that what he does is remotely okay?"

I watch in horror as her eyes change. So much like her brother's, they come alive when the rage courses through their veins. "This is the *bratva*. Here, women are not respected. We are tools. That is it. Why else do you think that I am being made to marry Alexei Dmitriev—your brother? My father would roll in his grave if he knew what my brother has done!"

I take a step back as my eyes grow wide. "Why would he have you marry Alexei?"

Alina scoffs. "Because your father is not a stupid man. He spoke with my brother, threatened to wage a war if the stakes weren't evened out. He figures if Dimitri has you, that they are to have me. I'm to become a *Dmitriev*. Something that I swore to never become."

"Well if it's any consolation, my family will never mistreat you as your brother has me."

She smirks as she steps towards me. "Do you think that they're innocent, Sofia? What do you think they do for a living? They *sell* women. They sell drugs … weapons. They are no different than this family. Alexei despises me. He doesn't want this. He's doing it because he's being forced to do it. Do you think that a man will be kind to a woman whom he's forced to marry?"

"Yes," I whisper. "He will be kinder than your brother has been to me."

Chapter 30

Promises to Keep

DIMITRI

I hum as I run my hand over the flesh where it hangs.

Taxidermy fascinates me. It's the process; peeling the skin away, preserving it, stuffing and mounting it. Though, this time is very different than the others. This time, it's pieces upon pieces of countless hunts that I'm putting together. Pieces that I've saved for this moment. Why hunt–why kill, if you're not to use the flesh?

I've been dreaming of this. To see what my hands are capable of, and to admire it as art.

No … not an animal, but the beauties who I tear apart in front of the camera. There are so many in this room. The flesh hangs as it tans beneath the UV lights. *My favorite parts of them.* I didn't like any one whole, I only liked pieces. Sofia, she's the only one who I want in her entirety. She is perfect in every way. From her flawless face to her beautiful round belly, all the way to her toes. I can't get enough of her.

When she has my perfect little baby, I can only imagine that she'll be even more beautiful. But I want more than just her beauty. I want her to accept me. To understand the workings of my mind. She doesn't of course. She doesn't want to understand what makes me tick. Because she's perfect, and I'm flawed. She sees me as a monster, and I see her as an angel. How are we ever to see eye to eye?

I hear someone approach the door, and I already know it's my sister by the sound of her heels clicking against the concrete.

"What do you want?" I snap without looking towards her.

"Please do not—"

"Enough!" I exclaim, turning to face her. "You will do what needs to be done for this family. Do you understand?"

I watch the tears rise to her eyes, but she quickly blinks them away. "Tell me. Tell me what I've done."

I sneer at her. "Alina, you are to marry Alexei, and you are to honor him by having a smile on your face when you do! Do you understand?"

She begins shaking her head emphatically. "No."

My chest heaves as I approach her, and she doesn't cower. She never does.

"*Yes*."

Alina sticks her chest out in defiance. "*No*."

She gasps when I tangle my fingers in her hair before yanking her head back. "You dare tell me no? You have no say in the matter. Now get the fuck out."

I release her and turn, but pause when I hear her words. "Whatever happened to us? To what we used to be?"

"I do not think two teenagers experimenting is considered *anything*." I rasp, trying to keep the memories from flickering through my mind, but I can't when I feel her hand creep up my back.

"I thought it *was* something."

I whip around to face her and grasp her wrist, squeezing it harshly and causing her to wince. "You never speak of those moments. Why now? Because you are afraid, Alina. Because you want to manipulate me … change my mind. That will not happen."

"You used me!" she wails, attempting to snatch her wrist from my grasp and failing. "You used me, and you're using me again."

I scoff. "*Used* you? Used you!" I force her onto her knees. "Go on. You want to stay here? You want to be my fuck toy until my wife is through carrying my child, do it. Show me now, Alina."

I stare down at her pathetic face as the tears stream down her cheeks. "No? But whatever happened to us, Alina? Tell me!"

"Fuck you!" she spits out, narrowing her eyes at me.

I smirk at her. "That's what I thought. Now get the fuck out. If I have to say it again, I'll shove my cock down your throat and remind you why we stopped in the first place."

She scurries from the room and I smile as I turn towards my workbench. I have a self-made mannequin for this piece, and this will not be my last. This is the first of many.

I do not have answers for my desires, nor do I wish to give them up. For Sofia, her escape is the ice—she almost allowed it to swallow her. Mine is here, below the surface of the dacha's wooden floors—killing, crafting, perfecting my art.

I saved her, but there's nobody saving me. It's how it's always been, and it's something that I've grown accustomed to. She may not be able to save me, but she is to stand by my side just as she vowed to do when she married me.

I pick up two pieces of flesh along with the hook needle that's been threaded with black thread. A good, sturdy needle is necessary in order to puncture the tough, tanned flesh. I begin humming again, and my mind goes to a peaceful place, where all I can think of is the needle as it weaves in and out of the skin.

I puff on my cigarette as I walk down the hall, stopping when I see my portrait in its respected place. What sacrifices am I to make as the Pakhan? What am I to lose? I've already lost my mind.

Sofia. Sofia and my child.

That's ultimately why I'm allowing Alexei to marry Alina. It's the only way to even out the playing field. It's the only way to keep them from Sofia.

Continuing on my way, I stop outside of our bedroom door. Every time that I'm to be with her, I have to pull myself back. I have to be the man she expects me to be. For her love … for her devotion. I can't be who I am when I'm below.

Once I enter, she isn't in bed. The bathroom door is open, so I quietly make my way inside. She's resting in the bath with white rose petals surrounding her as they float atop the water. Her long hair covers her swollen breasts, and the top of her growing belly bobbles in the water. Her head rests on the side of the bath and her eyes are closed.

"Hello, mouse," I whisper, kneeling down beside her and gently running a hand over her stomach.

"Hmm?" Her lazy eyes open up to meet mine.

"You fell asleep. Here, let us get you out of the bath and in bed."

"What is it?" Vlad implores as he looks over my newest contraption.

I smile, excited to tell him of my creation. "It's another tool for the videos. It works like a pendulum. The girl is to lie on the wooden platform where she will be strapped down. Each blade is heavy enough to swing effortlessly back and forth—but here is what sets it apart." I pause, walking around to the motor. "This control panel will allow us to lower the blades as they swing. I've managed to program it to not offset the swinging blades."

Vlad runs a hand over his head as he looks at me quizzically. "How did you figure this out?"

I smirk, tapping my temple with my index finger. "The mind is an incredible thing, my friend. Now, let us get started.

They are all so different, and my eyes always tend to zero in on their tiny imperfections: birthmarks, moles, freckles. Those tend to be my favorite parts to keep. This girl … I like her face and her hair—red and silky—while her pale cheeks are dusted with beautiful, pink freckles.

She will be perfect for my next project.

She's afraid. They all are, and I cannot blame them. Death is permanent. Though, I'd imagine after being locked in a cage for weeks, barely fed and hanging onto any last hope of life, that eventually they will succumb to the undeniable truth that they will die here.

Everyone gives up hope eventually. What's left after that? A fraction of what they once were. I like peeling their layers away, watching them depreciate as time ticks by. Time eventually becomes an old friend that you used to trust, only to discover that it was deceiving you all along. You hold on tight, until your fingertips hesitantly allow it to slip away. Time is all we've got in this life and when it's gone, it's gone. You eventually slip into the abysmal darkness, and it will never let you go.

Then you realize … time never existed.

So many people chase heaven. So many people lose themselves in the unknown. I prefer to keep myself in the here and now. Here, I can release myself into the wilderness that is my mind.

Sofia can't render me spineless here with her inexplicable beauty … with her pureness … with her perfectness. This place belongs to *me*. My darkness dwells here. There is no pretending about the man that I am. There is nothing ceasing my demented tendencies.

"Please…." The redhead moans as her head rolls from one side to the other.

Running a hand over her silky hair, my exposed cheek brushes against hers. "Nobody is ready to die."

A sob escapes her as I tighten the strap over one of her wrists. I nod to Vlad and Andrei who each grab one of the blades and hold them above their heads; Andrei at the foot, and Vlad at the head of the table. The hood that I wear hangs over my eyes and nose as I step behind the table where she lies.

The room illuminates with each flash of the camera as the film clicks on. Vlad and Andrei release each of the blades, and the swoosh sound fills the room each time the blades cross each other. I've yet to begin lowering the pivot; I'm relishing in her fear. Her screams are the sweetest song as her wide eyes try and follow each blade simultaneously.

My mouth curls into a smile as her lips begin moving rapidly to a whispered prayer. I can see her pulse beating erratically as she clenches her fists, awaiting the worst.

"Please!" She wails, "Please, I'll do anything." A mixture of tears and snot streams from her face to the wood below her trembling form.

I cock my head and look into her wide, green eyes. "Accept your fate," I whisper. Then, I press the button.

The pivot jumps to life before it starts lowering the blades to her abdomen. She begins shaking her head erratically as she cries out inexplicability.

Suddenly, the room goes black.

SOFIA

My chest heaves as I release the lever. I rest my hand on my stomach before sliding down the wall. My eyes grow wide when I hear Dimitri holler, followed by hurried footsteps. I hold my breath as they get closer. Once they've passed me, I make my way to the room where he had the girl.

The place is pitch black, and I use my hands and my memory to find her. Why did I follow him? Why did I allow my eyes to see his sick hands at work? I couldn't bare it. I couldn't let him kill that girl. She's young and beautiful. I'm sure she was the vibrant girl that I once was. Still, this isn't anything less than idiotic.

This could be suicide.

Once I locate the room, I hear her quivering breaths followed by the swooshing sounds of the blades as they still swing back and forth with force. Reaching my hands out in front of me, I finally grasp the edge of what I believe is the god awful table he has her strapped to. She begins whimpering loudly.

"Please, be quiet. I'm here to help you," I rasp. My hands quickly get to work locating the straps that are holding her down, ducking low to make sure that I don't get hit with a blade.

"Don't move," I whisper, removing what I believe to be the last strap. "The blades are still swinging. You don't even have an inch of wiggle room. Stay flat on your back and see if you can shimmy your way off of the table."

"O–okay," she whimpers.

"Be careful, but be quick. We don't have much time."

When she falls to the hard floor beside me, the lights cut back on.

"Well isn't this sweet," Dimitri says nonchalantly behind us.

I gather the girl into my arms and scoot to the furthest wall, shielding her as I narrow my eyes at him.

"She can't be any more than fifteen, sixteen years old Dimitri. Leave her be. Let her live."

He smirks at me as his men appear behind him. "Go fetch the girl."

I shake my head emphatically as my arms tighten around her naked form. "You're going to be a father. You've got to stop this. There are other ways. *Please*."

I glare at Vlad as he approaches me, and I struggle with everything in me to keep him from pulling the screaming girl from my grasp, but it's no use. I sob as Dimitri sits behind me on the floor and pulls me to his chest as Vlad and Andrei once again strap the girl down.

"Watch, mouse. This is what you came to see."

I shake my head as tears stream down my cheeks. "You're evil."

His chest rumbles against my back as he chuckles darkly. "Have I ever denied that?"

Dimitri never lets go as the camera once again comes to life. I gave the poor girl useless hope, and now she must be even more terrified than she was before.

When the blades begin lowering once more, I try and turn my face away, but Dimitri grasps my jaw forcing me to watch the bloody, horrific display. The blades begin to rip through her abdomen, sending chunks of flesh and organs flying across the cold room.

I gasp when the warm blood sprays across my cheek and leaks onto my bottom lip. The girl's screams subtly die along with her will to live. Her body jumps several times before she goes completely limp, and her head flops over to the side—confirming that she's succumbed to what I tried to save her from.

I watch in horror as Dimitri secures the metal cuff around my ankle. "You can't keep me chained to the bed. I'll go insane."

He laughs. "Good. Welcome to my world."

I sniffle as I run a hand over my bleary eyes. "You make those videos because you want to make them. You have enough money to stop producing them. I'm sure there are other ways to keep the bratva afloat."

"Do not tell me how to run this bratva, Sofia. Do not tell me how I should do *anything*. Do you understand?" he snaps, his eyes darting to mine. "A good wife minds the house … the children. Poverty is very much a reality in Russia. Be happy that your husband is doing what he must to support you … to make you happy. I've been trying, Sofia. You do not make it easy."

"I don't want to be here!" I holler, my voice strained as I grab at my hair. "I want to be home. I want to be in

America. I want to be with Mirna, I want—" I gasp when he strikes me, sending me to my side on the bed before wrapping my hair around his fist.

"I do not care what you *want*. I do not care what you *need*. Not anymore. I've stretched myself very thin to appease you. I have kept my demons below the floors of this dacha, only to return a different man to you. Because I *love* you! All because I finally found something that I didn't want to break. Everything else … everything else means nothing. But you—you mean the world to me, yet you push me further to the point of no return."

His grip loosens in my hair as his eyes stare into nothing. He's losing his mind, and he's taking me down with him. I'm no longer independent, and I should have known this all along.

I'm a part of his world. That's it. I no longer belong to myself. Here … here is where I am, and I'll rot away in his madness before I can ever save myself.

That's the power he has over me. That's my fate: to drown in his aberration.

Chapter 31

A Stormy Night

SOFIA

4 Months Later

I look out into the blizzard as my stomach tightens. *This is it.* I keep telling my baby to stay inside.

There isn't any power, and there aren't any doctors. I'm in labor, yet I haven't told a soul. Each time my womb constricts, I say a prayer. I'm silently suffocating—suffering. I don't want this. My baby is safe in my womb, but outside … he or she won't survive this.

They won't survive their father.

I've been chained to this bed for *months*. My ankle still bares the cuff that it has for so long, leaving a red mark around it. Seemingly, it's permanent; a reminder of the captive I am. Now, I'm to give birth in the same bed that this baby was conceived in.

My nose flares as I try and count my breaths, gripping my stomach in my palms as I try and stop the inevitable from happening; this baby is coming out, whether I want it to or not.

I've never known this type of pain. It feels like a million knives are stabbing my abdomen. I can't control it, as much as I try. It hurts unlike anything that I've ever felt. I fall to my knees and cry out when the liquid emerges from my womb. I tried to stay quiet, but it's impossible.

"*Sofia*!"

I know that voice. It's Vadim, once again saving me as he captures me beneath my arms.

Dimitri grasps my legs as they place me atop the mattress. My breaths are hurried as I try and keep myself from passing out. The pressure between my legs is more than I can bare. The baby's head presses against my cervix, and I cry out when it feels as if I'm being split open.

"Blood. All I can see is blood," Dimitri says, his voice quivering as he looks between my thighs.

"Pull it together, cousin. Your child will not survive if you do not."

I look towards Dimitri and watch as his wide gaze locks onto the middle of my thighs. His face is serious as he concentrates on the task at hand. I scream when I feel myself open up. I can't take my eyes away from my husband as he works on delivering our baby.

The pain is unimaginably unbearable … but then, I hear my baby. It screams towards the ceiling, and I smile when I look between my bloody thighs and see *her*. She's perfection.

Suddenly … *I fall in love.*

Dimitri leans forward and hands me my little girl. Her little eyes try and peer at me, and I can't help but run my index finger over her cheek. "Hello, sweet girl."

My eyes snap to Dimitri's. "Eva. I want to name her Eva."

He nods slowly, running a hand over his face and leaving a smear of my blood in its path. "Alright," he growls as he stands and begins walking towards the door, pausing before leaving the room. "We're going to try again very soon. I'd like a son."

Once he leaves, I remember that I'm still in Vadim's embrace.

"She's beautiful," he whispers against my cheek as I stare down at her.

I brush my cheek against his as I find his eyes. "She is," I murmur, pulling out my breast and helping her nurse. "She's perfection."

Vadim tightens his arms around me as I feed my child. His face rests against mine as a solitary tear creeps down my cheek.

She won't mean anything more than I do in Dimitri's eyes. She's weak, because she's like me.

My heart hurts for my daughter, in the worst way.

Chapter 32

Some Secrets are meant to be kept

DIMITRI

"Skazhite mne, kak tsifry," I murmur into the phone as I look outside.

Sofia is rocking our baby beneath a tree. Eva just turned two months old, and she's the perfect combination of her mother and me. Her hair is light brown, and her big brown eyes look so much like her mother's.

Sofia is a good mother. I was initially worried when she began acting mental, but she's doing an incredible job. She and Eva are like glue and, unfortunately, that has stolen precious time from my wife and me.

Never did I think that I would be jealous of my own child. Perhaps it is because she's a girl. If I had a son, I could teach him so many things; hunting and taxidermy … crafting. But lo and behold, Sofia has suddenly become infertile. We've tried and tried many times since the birth of our daughter to no avail.

I've asked the vrach why, but she has no answers other than, "Keep trying. Good things come to those who wait." She thinks that I'm insane for wanting another child so soon. I've considered putting her back on birth control since that seems the only way for her to become pregnant.

I make my way back to my desk and write down the numbers that Anatoly, our main drug dealer, says into the phone. I nod hastily as I plop into my chair and allow the pen to roll across the desk.

Hanging up the phone, I toss it onto my desk before relaxing in my chair. Just as I'm allowing myself to doze off, a knock sounds from my office door.

"What," I grit out, annoyed.

The door creaks open and Alina pokes her head in. "I wanted to come by and say hello to my *dear brother*."

I smile as she slinks her way in, closing the door behind her before sitting on the edge of my desk. "How is married life treating you, sister?"

Annoyance flashes across her face as she purses her lips. "Unlively. My husband is handsome, but he doesn't ever want to *fuck*."

Cocking my head, I regard my beautiful sister. When we were younger, I knew that it was wrong—but she was irresistible. I couldn't stop myself from going to her room at night … from using her.

"It's a shame," I murmur and her eyes flit to mine. "How can he *not* fuck you?"

Her spine straightens at my words, and lust immediately fills her cognac eyes. "He hates me."

"You're easy to hate," I retort, and she rolls her eyes.

"So are you."

I growl as I stand and approach her, sliding my hands up her thighs and taking her skirt with them. "Did you come here to berate me, little sister? I know you're angry that I had you marry him."

"Angry is an understatement," she rasps as I part her thighs, my lips hovering above hers.

"Tell me. Tell me how angry you are," I whisper, slipping my hand between her thighs.

She gasps when I begin circling her clit. "I–I…."

"Go on," I taunt as I pick up the speed. "Tell me how much you hate me."

A hushed moan escapes her lips when I slip a finger inside of her, slowly moving in and out, causing her back to arch. She grips my wrist and attempts to lead my movements, but I grasp her hand and pull it away.

"I'm going to fuck you one last time, Alina. Because the thought of fucking a woman who belongs to another man—to my enemy—it's enough to make my cock painfully hard."

Moving her panties aside, I free my erection before slamming into her, clamping my palm over her mouth to keep her quiet as I fuck her hard.

It doesn't take long for us to find our release. It never did. Because this is *forbidden*. This is *wrong*.

Resting my forehead against hers, I slowly pull out of her dripping pussy, but stop when I hear the door creak open. Alina's wide eyes lock onto the door behind me, and I slowly turn to see my younger cousin, Boris, frozen in place. I tuck my cock into my pants and take a step towards him.

"Hello, cousin."

He doesn't say a word. He turns and runs with all of his might, but I'm right on his tail, capturing him at the head of the stairs.

"Curiosity killed the cat," I whisper, before snapping his neck and slamming my foot into his back, sending him tumbling down the stairs.

"Dimitri," Alina whispers from behind me.

I shrug. "Some secrets are meant to be kept."

VADIM

"Vadim! I've been looking everywhere for you!" Alina exclaims as she enters my bedroom unannounced.

I've just stepped out of the shower and still have a towel wrapped around my waist.

"What is it? What's wrong?" I respond, noting her disheveled appearance.

"Boris, he fell down the stairs," she whimpers before she begins sobbing uncontrollably.

My back straightens. "Well? Is he alright?"

She shakes her head slowly. "I'm so sorry, Vadim. Boris is dead."

“The trauma to his neck isn’t consistent with a fall. It’s almost as if his neck was snapped clean in half.”

My eyes grow wide as I look down at my little brother’s cold, lifeless body. “So you’re saying that he didn’t fall down the stairs?”

The pathologist shakes his head as he rips the gloves from his hands before tossing them into the trash. “Oh, he fell down the stairs. Accidental? I wouldn’t say it was accidental.”

I frown. There is only one person that is capable of killing one of his own. There is only one person whose blood runs so cold.

“As usual, let’s keep this between us,” I murmur, slipping him a wad of rubles. “I’ll figure out who did this to Boris.”

He purses his lips as he snatches the money from my hand. “I’ll take it that this won’t be the last body that I’ll see?”

I cover my brother with the sheet and sigh, running a hand down my face. “You know the deal, Igor. No questions.”

I stop outside of the examiners office and light a cigarette. The loss of my brother hurts. I’ve witnessed too many people that I loved die because of the bratva.

My daughter … my brother …. When does it become too much? Why can't I shed tears for my brother's demise? I've asked myself that question a thousand times on my way to speak to the examiner. I knew that Boris didn't trip down those stairs and die as a result. I felt it when I saw his twisted body at the foot of the stairs, and I knew that familiar look in Dimitri's eye.

It was the same look that he had when Dyadya Albert died. He doesn't know of my relationship with the examiner, about our understanding. I know the truth about what happened to Dyadya Albert.

Dimitri is arrogant. He likes to think that he's sneaky, but he isn't. I learned how to read him a very long time ago—when he began to worry me. Now, I'm afraid that the next cold body I'll be staring down at will be Sofia's. I need to find out what Dimitri is trying to hide.

There are only two reasons why he'd want Boris dead: revenge or to keep a secret.

And I'm going with the latter.

SOFIA

“Hello, my little ray of sunshine,” I whisper as Eva’s little eyelids peer open. “You were sleeping so well, but you need to eat.”

Lifting her from her crib, I pull out my swollen breast. Eva immediately latches on, and I sway back and forth as she nurses.

“Your grandmother would be swept away with your beauty, little one.”

I hear Dimitri clear his throat and turn to face him. “I’m almost done feeding her if you’d like to hold her.”

He nods and sits in the rocking chair, watching me as I continue to hum to Eva.

“Boris is dead,” he murmurs, and my eyes snap to his.

“Dead? What happened?”

Dimitri sighs, running a hand down his face. “He took a bad fall down the stairs and broke his neck.”

I shake my head slowly as the tears rise in my eyes. The boy from the village … the one with curious eyes … *dead.* He was never like the others. Like me, he never belonged in this place.

“Is Vadim okay?”

Dimitri scoffs. "Not a single tear from him. The man wouldn't know sorrow if it bit him."

"That's not true," I retort, and Dimitri's eyes snap to mine.

"Is she about done? I need to get some more work done."

I nod and pull her from my breast before burping her and handing her to her father.

She looks so small wrapped in his muscular arms. She's never cracked a smile in his presence, not once. I'm hoping that will change soon.

"She always frowns at me," Dimitri mutters as he stares down at her. "Why won't she smile?"

I smile slightly as I approach them and kneel down at his feet. "Play with her. Sing to her. She likes that."

His brow furrows. "That's a mother's job."

"And a father's," I whisper, placing a hand over his.

His gaze flits to mine momentarily before it snaps back to her. "In Russia, mothers will sing songs to their children to warn them of death, starvation, and wolves."

I watch him as a slight smile curls his lips, his index finger runs gently over Eva's soft cheek.

“Why do you stand, swaying oh slender birch tree, with your head bent to your very stem? But across the road—across a wide river—similarly lonely, stands a tall oak tree. How can I birch tree, clamber over to the oak tree? I wouldn’t bend and sway as I do now, I wouldn’t bend and sway as I do now. With my slender branches, I would lean against him. And with his foliage, I would whisper day and night.”

My heart soars when I see Eva’s toothless smile as she stares up at her father. Dimitri’s eyes fill with tears for a split second, but then they’re gone. A tiny glimmer of hope, that’s all he ever gives me. That is the most hope that he’s ever given Eva. Just like that, her smile turns into a frown and I watch them stare into each other’s eyes with such misunderstanding. It’s more than I can take.

“That was beautiful,” I whisper, snapping Dimitri out of his daze.

“I must go now,” he murmurs, leaning forward and placing Eva into my arms before his lips find mine. “Tonight, me and you. I need you.”

I nod as he swiftly stands and leaves me and our daughter alone once more.

“This is really nice,” I murmur as I stare across the intricately decorated table. Dimitri is handsome as ever, wearing a perfectly tailored black suit, no tie, and several buttons left unbuttoned to display his collarbone. His hair is unkempt as usual, but that only adds to his allure.

“I am glad that we’ve found time to be alone. I’ve missed you, mouse.”

I shake my head as he pours me some cabernet. Pushing it away, my eyes meet his. “I can’t drink. The baby, she’s still nursing.”

He cocks his head. “And?”

“Well,” I begin hesitantly, “What I consume, she consumes.”

I divert my eyes when I see that familiar fire glow in his gaze.

“Sofia, drink the wine,” he snaps, and I blink several times.

“But—” I jump when his fist slams into the table.

“Drink. The. Wine.”

I nod hastily as I pick up the glass with my trembling hand before taking a small sip. Dimitri’s fist is still balled tightly atop the table, but it begins to loosen.

"I hate having that tone with you. You need to start listening."

"You seem tense," I whisper, avoiding his eyes.

"Do I?" he states, sarcastically. "Funny you should say that, because I am a little tense. I'm a little tense because it seems that my wife has forgotten her husband when she became a mother."

"I–I didn't. I'm sorry that you feel that way. I'm trying," I whisper, my eyes finding his as they brim with tears. "I'll try harder."

He lets out a long sigh as he relaxes in his seat. "I'd like for us to have a night alone, Sofia. Let the nanny take care of Eva. Let us be together. Let us drink and *fuck*."

"She's never been with the nanny. She'll be terrified," I whisper, but I know that I can't go any further. I know it will do no good as I watch his fist tighten once more. "But you're right," I say hurriedly. "We do need to spend time together. I'm sure Eva will be fine."

"Good," he says nonchalantly. "I'm looking forward to it."

I nod slowly before pushing my food around with my fork. "I liked seeing you and her together today. It was nice."

He exhales sharply before stabbing the meat with his fork. "*Enough* about Eva."

My nostrils flare and the blood in my veins runs hot at his words. *Enough about Eva?* How dare him. How dare he ignore the sweet angel that somehow rose from the ashes of my soul and brought me back to life. Eva is the only thing that holds my heart. She's the only thing keeping me alive. She is the only thing that makes me happy. I'd forgotten what happiness was until I saw her smiling face. I'd forgotten how beautiful life can be after everything.

Those last months of my pregnancy chained to the bed sunk me into the lowest depths of depression. I never thought that such sadness was possible. I couldn't comprehend ever finding happiness again … until *her*. It's becoming clearer each day that Dimitri despises my happiness. He feeds off of my sadness, just like he feeds off of my fear. It ignites the demon in him. It nourishes his chaotic mind.

"Why don't you love our daughter?" I snap. "She's just a baby. You've never given her a chance!"

Dimitri bares his teeth, and his eyes shimmer with ill will. He leans forward, his face distorting into absolute hatred, causing a cold shiver to run down my spine. "Understand this—and I refuse to sugarcoat it for you, *my love*—but you are *mine*. I chose you. You chose me, remember? Do you remember our vows? Do you remember your promise to me?"

"And she's your daughter," I retort, rising to my feet. "We made her. I thought that's what you wanted. I thought that you wanted me in every way—your wife, your submissive, and your frightened little mouse … the mother of your child! What else can I give you? Tell me!"

He grips the table as he slowly stands, growing taller and more intimidating by the second. I scream when he knocks the dishes from the table and stalks towards me.

"Don't hurt me," I whisper as I cower, the remnants of my soul shrivel at the sound of my pleading voice.

"You fucking bitch," he sneers. "I should have left you below, in the cage. I should have let you *die*."

"Dimitri," I whisper as he backs me against the wall.

"You make me so angry! How do you do that? How do you get in my head, Sofia?" he hollers, tapping his temple with his index finger.

"I–I don't know. I don't try to, Dimitri. Please—"

My words are cut off when he wraps his fingers around my neck, squeezing tightly and cutting off my oxygen. The blood rises to my face as my fingers try to pry his hand away. My eyes are wide as tiny stars dance in front of my vision, the pressure from the lack of oxygen is unbearable. All I can see is Eva. And to think, months ago I wanted nothing but to leave this earth.

When I think that my eyes will pop out of their sockets as a result of the pressure, he releases me. I crumple to the floor and cough excessively as I grab at my throat. Dimitri grabs a handful of my hair before yanking me to my feet and slamming me onto the table. He grasps my shirt and yanks it from my body effortlessly before doing the same to my bra. My engorged breasts are sore. Eva should be feeding right now.

He squeezes them harshly, and I writhe as the breastmilk leaks from my nipples Leaning down, he takes my nipple into his mouth before biting down, causing me to cry out. Then he begins sucking. I try to push him away, but it's no use.

"Please. Please stop, that's Eva's!" I cry out between sobs, but he doesn't stop.

I feel my breast drain of my daughter's nourishment before he moves on to the other and does the same. Time ticks by slowly, and my tears never let up when he yanks the yoga pants down my legs before shoving into me. I scream from a mixture of pain and frustration as he grips my wrists above my head and holding me down as he once again uses my body.

I kick and slap as Dimitri once again chains me to the bed. I don't have any leeway like before. Before, I could freely move about the room, but not anymore. The worst part, I haven't a clue where my daughter is. She won't survive without me.

"Eva!" I cry out when he turns and begins walking from the room. He stops momentarily before continuing on his way, leaving me alone.

I curl into a ball, holding my knees against my chest as each uncontrollable sob bubbles from my chest.

I'm starving to death. I'm barely clinging on. My breasts have dried out. I haven't seen my daughter in .... I've lost count of the days, the hours, the minutes. I'll die here, and that means that she'll die, too.

VADIM

I watch the dancer circle the pole to a song that I swore I'd never listen to again.

I'm losing the battle between right and wrong. I don't know where I go from here. Sweet Sofia … or the family that I've known through every hardship.

The dancer crawls towards me as I take a deep drawl from my cigarette. Her bottom lip hangs down as she slinks towards me like a kitten. She's far too skinny. Her hip bones protrude, threatening to break through the skin, and her ribs cannot be missed. Her face is pretty, though it's rather skeletal. She lacks Sofia's soft curves … her inner indecisiveness that I crave like nothing else. This dancer is a shell. Sofia is the entire package. Pure perfection.

Mine.

"The car is waiting."

The whisper in my ear doesn't catch me off guard. I know where I'm to go. I know what I'm to do.

I slide into the back of the car and look towards the shadow that sits across from me. "My snova vstrechayemsya." *We meet again.*

I nod. "I would like to help you. Sofia is very dear to me. I wish for her to be free of my cousin."

Chapter 33

A Taste of Freedom

SOFIA

My vision is blurry as my eyes peel open, and my ears ring from what sounds like an alarm. Hurried voices … hurried footsteps. Absolute chaos.

I try and lift my head, but I can't. My strength has diminished more and more each day that I've been locked away naked, starved, and dehydrated. It feels like I've been here for weeks, but I can't be certain.

My eyes flutter shut once more, and I listen as the door splinters open. I feel the cuff loosen around my ankle before strong arms wrap around me, lifting my body. I whimper as my head rolls to the side.

"It's okay, krasavaya. It's all going to be okay."

I part my lips to speak, but my tongue is so dry; my lips cracked. Reaching out, I run a hand over Vadim's rough cheek as the sounds from outside of the room become more evident. I try to open my eyes several times and each time I do, all I can see are flashes of people as they run by us, hollering in Russian.

Before I know it, my body is shivering excessively. I believe that we're outside, but the next second I am warm once more and something soft is wrapped around my body. Then, I feel like I'm moving, but sedentary. I must be inside of some type of vehicle.

I feel a hand run over my hair, and when I open my eyes, I see a familiar face.

"Papa," I whisper as I stare up into his sad eyes.

"Sleep now, Sofia. All is well."

I nod slowly before closing my eyes once more.

I keep hearing Eva. She's crying, but I'm stuck with nothing holding me down. I try screaming her name, but I have no voice. The walls begin closing in on me. Once a room, I'm now trapped in a narrow hallway. All I can see ahead is darkness. Then I hear footsteps, and I see Eva dangling as Dimitri holds her up by her ankle. I keep hearing a dripping sound, and then I see its source. Eva is bleeding from her neck. When my eyes

travel up, I see Dimitri with an evil grin covering his face.

"Look, mouse. Look at your daughter."

I gasp, darting up into a sitting position as my heart threatens to beat out of my chest. My body is covered in sticky sweat. I hold a hand out in front of me, peering through my fingers as the sunlight floods through the window.

I hear a beeping sound and my eyes travel to a machine. My eyes follow the slender tube and I lift my hand, observing the IV before I take in the rest of the room. I don't believe that I'm in a hospital. I'm in a cozy room decorated in soft whites and browns.

The large window displays a beautiful, blue sky. I slide my legs off the bed and use the machine to balance as I stand on shaking legs. It takes several steps for me to make my way to the window, and when I look out the scenery takes my breath away. The water is almost turquoise as the white waves roll to the shore. Palm trees are swaying in the breeze, and the white sand looks so welcoming.

"You're awake."

I whip around to face the voice. "Vadim," I whisper. "Where am I?"

He approaches me, standing beside me as he stares out the window. "Sochi."

I sigh as my eyes travel back to the window. "Where is Eva? Please tell me that she's okay."

"Eva is napping. She's alright."

I grasp at my chest as tears pour from my eyes. "My baby. I need to see her."

Vadim wraps an arm around my waist before leading me to the bed. "She'll be here as soon as she's done with her nap. She's very cranky when you interrupt her beauty sleep."

I laugh through the tears as he helps me sit on the edge of the bed. "You saved us. Thank you."

He sits beside me before gently running his fingers over my cheek. "I didn't do it alone. Your father and brother were instrumental in your rescue."

"How can I ever repay you?" I whisper as I stare up into his eyes.

He sighs, looking away quickly. "You said it yourself. I owe you my life."

"Now we're even," I whisper, and his lips curl into a smile.

"Yes, krasavaya. We're even."

Two Weeks Later

I smile as I look into Eva's sweet, brown eyes. "You were a hungry girl," I whisper, pulling the bottle from her lips and propping her up on my knee, alternating between rubbing and patting her back to burp her.

Once I lay her down, I gently close the door to her room to avoid waking her. I smile when I see Vadim standing in the living room, his back facing me as he stares out the window.

"Hi," I whisper, and he turns to face me.

"I wanted to come and see how you and Eva are doing."

Walking to the couch, I sit and curl my legs under me before patting the space beside me. Once he sits, I prop my cheek on my knuckles as I stare at his handsome, rugged face.

"You haven't been here in a few days."

"I've been busy," he murmurs, his eyes flitting to mine. "I've been meaning to, I promise. If I could be here every day, I would."

"I get so scared," I mutter. "Every sound that I hear has me on edge. When you're not here, I feel so vulnerable."

"Things will change soon. Right now, we have to be careful. That's why you're at this hotel and not with your family."

"When will I see them?"

He looks into my eyes as he leans his head against the back of the couch. "Soon," he whispers, placing a hand over my cheek.

I sigh as I press my cheek against his palm, and his eyes gloss over as he regards me. I can feel his desire in the air, and my own matches his. I want him. I've *wanted* him for so long.

Reaching over, I slip my hand between the buttons of his white dress shirt and he squeezes his eyes shut. "Sofia…"

"Stay with me tonight."

His eyes snap open and they are filled with imminent desire. "If I stay, then I will not be able to leave."

"Then don't leave," I rasp, straddling him on the couch before I grind against his erection.

"Sofia," he rasps as he grabs my hips, his fingers digging into my flesh.

I frantically unbutton his shirt, displaying the many tattoos that mar his skin. His chest is defined and strong, and I can't help but trail kisses from his neck to his pecs. He pulls my nightgown over my head before he grasps my breasts and squeezes gently.

"I have been waiting for this moment … thinking that it would never happen."

"Me too," I whisper, rocking against his length once more.

He grasps my back, cradling me against him as he lays me down and brushes his nose against mine. "You have awoken the man that I buried long ago. I will not ever let you go, krasavaya."

My eyes flutter open and I listen to the steady beat of Vadim's heart as I rest my cheek against his naked chest. Our legs are entwined as he holds me close. Clothing litters the floor of the living room and the sunlight inches across the floor as the sun rises over the ocean.

I try and inch my way off of the couch, but his arm tightens around me. “Good morning.”

I smile as I look into his eyes. “Good morning.”

“Today, I must get some things taken care of. It will take several hours. Will you be alright?”

I nod before pressing my lips to his.

“I’ll be fine.”

“Goodbye,” Vadim whispers before kissing my forehead. “Tonight, we’ll order some dinner. Maybe watch a movie.”

I nod. “Okay.”

Once he leaves, I smile before looking at the clock. Eva needs to wake up from her nap. I turn and begin making my way to the door to the room that she sleeps, but stop when I hear a light knock on the door. Smiling, I make my way to the door.

“Did you forget something?” I say jokingly as I swing the door open, but nobody is there.

I look up and down the vacant hall, and my eyes snap to a small, brown object a ways down the hall.

I tiptoe to it and gasp at what I find: a small, dead mouse.

I turn and hurry my way back to the door, slamming it shut and locking each lock. Backing away slowly, my heart beats erratically beneath my ribs. My back hits something hard, and before I can say a word, a hand slaps over my mouth.

"I've missed you mouse."

TO BE CONTINUED…

SNUFF (Book 2)

Coming summer 2016

This time, when the vehicle pulls up to the Vavilov dacha, it's different. I know my fate, and as I clutch Eva against my chest – I wonder how long I'll be able to hold onto her before she's taken away too.

Dimitri sits across from me in the limo, his fingers curled around his knees and his knuckles turning white. His eyes hold a promise. They hold no hope. They assure malevolence.

I'm to suffer for my departure.

I'm to suffer for being with Vadim.

Time has no relevance here. Time ticks away, and it will never return.

Dimitri's eyes have not left mine, and my gaze matches his dare. I got a taste of freedom. I haven't tasted it in so long. He has me now.

Now… but I've survived for this long. I've made it this far, and I do not intend on giving up.

When the limo rolls to a stop, he nods to the door once the driver opens it, and he follows behind me once I exit the vehicle. I walk in stride, putting one foot after the other with my head held high.

Eva doesn't make a sound as she clutches my collar in her tiny hand.

Upon approaching the double doors to the dacha, they open up seemingly by themselves. Dimitri's staff and men await us as I climb the steps to the hell that I've come to know so well.

The nanny that had cared for Eva extends her arms, and I look down at my baby, kissing her forehead gently… allowing the tender kiss to last, because I don't know when I will see her again.

"Stay alive for me, sweet girl, and I promise I will do the same." I whisper against her cheek before she's taken from my arms. My hands fall to my sides when the nanny turns with my little girl, the others following in suit.

Dimitri appears beside me, his shoulder touching mine. "You have diminished any chance of freedom, Sofia. You've betrayed me, and I'm afraid there is no coming back from that. You thought that your life was hell before… I'm afraid that your hell has just begun."

I clench my jaw when I feel his gaze fall upon me. The embers that are his eyes burn holes into my very flesh.

"I want you to get on your hands and knees and *crawl.* Whether or not you're in my presence, you are never to walk amongst me or within the walls of this dacha on your feet again. You are *filth.* You betrayed me, and if I wasn't a better man than my father – I would strangle every ounce of life from you."

father – I would strangle every ounce of life from you."

About the Author

Bonny Capps was born in Rowlett, Texas, but lived most of her life in the Galveston Gulf Coast area. Bonny was home schooled by her mother and this is where she developed her love for writing. Her first attempts at writing were in the form of poetry. Bonny married her longtime boyfriend Dusty Capps in 2014. They have two boys Mitch 11 years old and Damon 8 years old. In 2014 Bonny and the boys decided to leave their home behind and join Dusty on the road in his semi-truck and have traveled throughout the United States. It was during this once in a life time adventure that Bonny found her voice and began to write Dark Erotica. Her first dark erotic book, Deliverance for Amelia is a best seller in the U.S. and U.K. Bonny has received rave reviews and is excited to have released the third and final book in the Killer Series.

Upcoming books are SNUFF (book 2) and Seven Fears, which will be released in 2016!

She will also be co-writing "Twins" with Tara Dawn, and that will be released this Fall.

Follow me on Facebook:

www.facebook.com/bonnycappsauthor

Or Twitter:

@BonnyC_Author

Order signed books on my website:

http://bonnycappsauthor.vpweb.com/

Join the club for updates:

https://www.facebook.com/groups/810154955767136/

CPSIA information can be obtained
at www.ICGtesting.com
Printed in the USA
LVHW081318210921
698357LV00011B/223